Girl's Girl

Girl's Girl

| *a novel* |

Sonia Feldman

THE DIAL PRESS
NEW YORK

The Dial Press
An imprint of Random House
A division of Penguin Random House LLC
1745 Broadway, New York, NY 10019

randomhousebooks.com
penguinrandomhouse.com

LIBRARY OF CONGRESS CATALOGING-IN-PUBLICATION DATA
Names: Feldman, Sonia (Novelist) author
Title: Girl's girl: a novel / Sonia Feldman.
Description: First edition. | New York, NY: The Dial Press, 2026.
Identifiers: LCCN 2025038072 (print) | LCCN 2025038073 (ebook) |
ISBN 9780593978924 hardcover | ISBN 9780593978931 ebook
Subjects: LCGFT: Bildungsromans | Novels | Fiction
Classification: LCC PS3606.E3867 G57 2026 (print) |
LCC PS3606.E3867 (ebook)
LC record available at https://lccn.loc.gov/2025038072
LC ebook record available at https://lccn.loc.gov/2025038073

Printed in the United States of America

3rd Printing

Book team: Production editor: Luke Epplin • Managing editor: Rebecca Berlant • Production manager: Ali Wagner • Copy editor: Kathy Lord • Proofreaders: Taylor McGowan, Liz Carbonell, Tricia Wygal

Book design by Susan Turner

The authorized representative in the EU for product safety and compliance is Penguin Random House Ireland, Morrison Chambers, 32 Nassau Street, Dublin D02 YH68, Ireland.
https://eu-contact.penguin.ie

There are only a few times in life when we think we are going to live forever. And I think one of them is when we are with our friends, laughing, eating, looking each other in the eye.

—Mary Ruefle, "Dear Friends"

Girl's Girl

GROWING UP, I HAD TWO BEST FRIENDS—MARGARET, WHOM I HAD known my whole life, and Eleanor, with whom I was in love, though for years I had no reason to tell my feelings for one apart from my feelings for the other. Both were fervent.

Eleanor asked me for advice about her Sims, then never took it. Margaret asked me in which of a series of nearly identical photos I thought her boobs looked best for the internet, so I told her. I kept the clothes Eleanor lent me for too long, and I kept the clothes Margaret lent me for too long. Eleanor didn't borrow anybody's clothes, and Margaret never gave mine back at all.

We chose each other's outfits. We slept in each other's beds. I had a near constant awareness of both my friends as existing in parallel to myself. And that awareness became tender when we were apart, painful when I was apart from them and they were not apart from each other. This happened often enough. They both had a great deal more freedom than I did. Margaret because she was lawless and Eleanor because her parents never made any laws.

Until the summer before our sophomore year of high school, I thought my love for Eleanor was my love for Margaret. Distinctions between ways of loving are fuzzy, and I couldn't name them, didn't even know I felt them, and least of all suspected I would soon ruin my life learning to distinguish them—learning I wanted more than one way to love my friends.

ON AN EARLY, EMPTY AFTERNOON IN JUNE, I TOLD MY MOM I NEEDED to walk over to Margaret's house. I didn't explain my urgency because if I said I had to hear Margaret's gossip in person, she'd ask me what the gossip was about.

At fifteen, I was allowed to walk most places. Doan, our neighborhood in the upper-right-hand corner of Ohio, was residential, majority populated by white people, the neighbors all apparently heterosexual. Massive hundred-year-old trees lined its streets, announcing stable affluence. A number of main boulevards stroked through the neighborhood in straight, cardinal directions. Between them ran a network of snaking circuitous avenues that met in irregular, asterisk-like intersections. Cars often lingered too long at stop signs, uncertain who held the right of way. None of these things prevented my mother from being afraid for me all the time, though I was aware that was their purpose. I didn't know how to accommodate her fear, and I didn't know how to assess its validity. Very few bad things had ever happened to me. She saw precarity where other people's parents seemed to see regular life. But then, she was smarter than everyone else. There was no one I trusted more than I trusted her.

The walk to Margaret's took between five and ten minutes depending on my mood. My mood depended on the weather. The weather that day was humid, my pace languorous. Dense air blurred my skin with sweat by the time I arrived at her house, a friendly rectangular building with a large front yard and a screened-in porch out back. The porch was old and heavily used, with mesh panels for walls that bowed outward like the knees of well-loved pants. I walked directly up the driveway to the back of the house and opened the screen door.

Margaret lay face down on the large white wicker couch in the middle of the room with her shirt off and her chestnut hair pushed up above her head, so it fell over the edge of the armrest. Eleanor straddled her back, her legs folded on either side of Margaret's bare torso. Bent over, her face hovered inches above Margaret's skin, a tissue fixed between her fingers. I raised my phone to take a picture of them. Margaret held up a thumb. Eleanor righted herself at the sight of me.

"Totally standard," I said with pleased sarcasm.

"As usual," Margaret sang.

Eleanor extracted a pimple from Margaret's right shoulder blade using her gel-polished fingernails and dismounted. Margaret pulled her shirt back on. I sat down in an adjacent chair. The porch looked like every other space in Margaret's house, crowded with belongings and evidence of feminine inhabitation. Spare cushions sat in tipping piles pushed up against the room's mesh perimeter. Potted plants on stands dripped green vines onto the tiled floor, and baskets of decade-old magazines featured the faces of girls we knew only as the women they'd become and instructions about sex we recognized as outdated but couldn't help occasionally reading aloud to each other in the guise of a joke.

"Mar refused to tell me anything until you got here, no previews, even though you've already heard," Eleanor complained.

She removed herself to the far side of the couch and sat

down with her legs folded beneath her, her elbow on the armrest and her pointed chin in her hand.

"Mar needs her whole audience—" I said.

"—and phone tellings only half-count," Margaret finished, her skin dewy with sweat and the pleasure of having gathered us for a purpose.

Margaret had recently given head for the first time. Hence my need to come over right away, lest she tell Eleanor in person without me. Neither of us had ever made it past anybody's pants. Margaret's having done so seemed a near mythical achievement, an announcement of the dawning of a new era of our lives in which we might possibly put our hands and mouths on the bodies of other people. Because she did things first among us. She did them on purpose, and she did them repeatedly in order to get better. She'd climbed in and out of all the possible second-story windows of her house before she'd ever had reason to use them.

Oral sex represented a box that she had wanted to check, so she checked it with a boy who went to a different school than us, who was good-looking but not importantly so, who was seventeen and therefore would go to college in a year and forget that Margaret existed. All of these attributes qualified him for a contained life experience, an experience whose significance would be determined by Margaret. If she didn't tell anyone, no one would know. Well, we would know, but we wouldn't tell anyone else because the only people we needed to tell anything to were each other.

"Wait," I said.

I wanted to see a picture of him first. I'd seen pictures of him before, but I wanted to remember exactly who I was supposed to imagine being fellated. Also, the request lent an air of pomp and circumstance to the telling, which was our preference—anything to enhance our sense of life as genuinely underway instead of just preparing to be. Eleanor pulled up his profile and handed her phone to me because if we let Margaret choose the photo it would take twenty minutes. Eleanor's oval nails had tiny rhinestones glued into sky-blue polish. She'd painted them herself. She could be very patient in pursuit of getting what she wanted, the way she wanted it.

"He doesn't photograph well," Margaret said, the standard caveat.

"Boys never do," I answered.

I slunk down into the chair. I was tall for my age, my arms and legs long. In this weather, they felt heavy. I used my elbows to prop my hands and the phone just a few inches from my face while I scrolled.

Margaret felt exposed by this moment of judgment and so began to tell Eleanor what she'd already told me, that one of her hundred and five thousand friends other than us had said that one of her friends had said that the boy had a normal penis.

"Which I found comforting in the lead-up, but also like, how do I know that she knows what's a normal dick? I don't. However, I can now report that it was fine, a totally nice starter penis."

"Great news," Eleanor said. "Thrilled to hear it."

Eleanor often sounded sarcastic both when she did and didn't mean something—a point of pride for her, the control of tone, the possibility of a private humor, which I found to be either annoying or delicious.

While they spoke, I scrolled. Pictures of the sky took up half the boy's profile, but a series of group photos revealed a tall, slim boy with shaggy hair, most often wearing a hunter-green bucket hat with a white swirl embroidered on the front. He could have been better-looking and he could have been worse. The main thing was that he had the bearing of a teenage boy who had definitely already hooked up with at least five total people, which limited risk of a certain variety. A baseline of experience existed.

Having gotten an impression, I closed the app and opened the front-facing camera. My oval face and my large dark eyebrows appeared on Eleanor's screen. I lowered my eyelashes and took several flattering photos of myself, my expression blank and my gaze directed first at the aperture, then beyond the phone toward my friends on the couch, Margaret still going on with her prelude about how she and this boy originally started texting, and then one last picture looking back down at the screen again with my eyes widened in jest and acknowledgment. I left these for El to find later, a game we sometimes played with each other, and flicked out of the application. It occurred to me again that I myself had almost no baseline of experience. No one could count on me to do anything first. I gave the phone back to Eleanor, who extended her hand, her nails winking in the muted light.

"Okay, he's hot, we're ready," I said.

Margaret nodded seriously and moved on to the most suggestive aspect of context, the real start of the story, which she had withheld telling until she had both our full attention. The boy's previous girlfriend had refused the act point-blank, and her denial filled Margaret with a feeling of superiority, a sense of her own sexual bravery.

"Are you really going to go your whole life without putting anyone's penis in your mouth?" Margaret asked with a flourish of the hand. "No—so I don't understand her reasoning."

In the lead-up, Margaret had experimented with bananas. The bananas were overripe and kept breaking apart in her mouth. She also watched a lot of porn.

"I searched for head tutorials online and the results were frankly—" She paused to make a face. "I thought I'd prefer to watch real people instead of porn stars, but real people are horrifying. The professionals were much more civilized."

"Where did you go to watch it?" Eleanor asked.

Margaret twisted the stack of woven and metal bracelets around her wrist.

"I don't know," she said, though of course she did know. "I started looking and it was there."

"But where specifically?"

"Well, in the search results," Margaret said.

"That's not an answer."

I cut them both off. "It's fine. Mar doesn't want us to retrace her exact horny internet steps. Keep going."

I loved listening to Margaret's stories, as though she were somehow both a salacious audiobook and a parent reading me to sleep.

She gave me a grateful blink.

The boy had picked her up in his car and driven them to the mall parking lot.

"His car smelled like boy body spray, but I was basically into that."

In the version of the story she'd told me over the phone, there had been an awkward conversation between the two of them in the parking lot before they climbed into the blanket-lined trunk of his car. But this time, he had a visible erection while they drove. The preamble to the act disappeared. They parked. She began. She described how she'd felt a painful awareness of her entire body, of her arms and legs and where they were and her teeth and hands and mouth and the slow passage of time. She hadn't been sure how long it would take, and she couldn't say with certainty how long it had taken. The boy had made a series of wonderful, unguarded breathy sounds as she continued her rhythm, which she tried to maintain as a continuous beat. In the aftermath, she'd asked the boy for specific feedback, which he gave stumblingly and without the use of a single anatomical word.

"He said I was good—" Margaret began.

"I'm sure you were," I interrupted, and El echoed, "Obviously."

"—and that he liked it when I used my hand and my mouth at the same time, like in the same rhythm," Margaret finished.

We nodded. This seemed like reasonable guidance.

Eleanor wanted more information about the boy's testicles.

"Did you do anything to them?" she asked.

"Absolutely not," Margaret said with a confidence born from resentment. She disliked the implication that she might be anything other than at ease with male anatomy. If she hadn't caressed any testicles, it certainly wasn't because she didn't know how to do so, Eleanor! And shouldn't we be dwelling on all she had achieved instead of pointing out what she hadn't? Margaret always wanted us to be proud of her. She wanted us to be grateful for her service in being the first of us, so that we could be the second and third, armed with the knowledge of her experience. "One thing at a time, okay!"

"I mean, I definitely don't think you have to," I said.

"Me neither," Eleanor agreed, sensing she'd pushed enough.

We offered this reassurance based on zero expertise, but it seemed likely to be true given that she hadn't and he still came.

Margaret resumed her story. As they left, a hint of danger—a mall cop who had rolled down his driver-side window to give them a look that said he knew they hadn't gone shopping. This was new. I hadn't heard it over the phone. I didn't know whether or not it had happened, though obviously Margaret included the detail in that moment to regain our reverence.

She never demonstrated any self-consciousness about the evolving details of her stories. We had a truce about the truth, the two of us. Margaret who slipped and skirted, and I who couldn't lie, who struggled even to evade—me with all my feelings always written on the surface of my body, with my self-serious sense of duty, of what was owed to the people I loved and what was owed to me by those who loved me in return.

Margaret wasn't a liar exactly, but she dispersed the truth unevenly and to her own advantage. The version of the story she told Eleanor was nearly identical to the version she had already told me, but the soft pencil of confusion and embarrassment that had shaded her first telling was erased and overwritten here. When they got back to her house, she'd given the boy a brief kiss on the cheek because she wasn't sure if it was rude to kiss him on the mouth, and then afterward regretted the decision and concluded that anyone whose penis she was kissing, she would thereafter kiss on the lips. And she was so committed to this adjustment in future behavior, so convinced that it was how she would always act from then on, that when she told Eleanor the story, it became the way she had already acted. Our eyes met as she said so, that she'd kissed him on the lips, but neither of us flickered.

A laden breeze shifted through the room.

Above me, the gossamer strands of a spiderweb bowed, glinting iridescently.

I lifted my hair from my neck for relief from the humidity.

With Margaret's core story told, we were free to pursue its radiating lines of inquiry. Whether or not she wanted to hook up with him again, for instance. Her desire to continue texting him whenever it suited her self-esteem. Eleanor brought up that she'd heard from one of her older sisters that one of their friends was allergic to semen. The girl had found this out through a trial-and-error situation. Antihistamines eventually solved the problem but only after it terrified all parties involved. Was there in fact a way to discover you were allergic to semen before the substance was trying to close one opening of yours or another? Not that we could think of, an alarming possibility. Margaret at least could now feel secure in her own non-reaction.

"Though I slept for like twelve hours that night," she said.

Eleanor and I gave her a simultaneous look.

"That is literally in no way an allergic reaction," I responded at the same time as Eleanor asked, "Do you know what an allergy is?"

"Lol maybe," Margaret answered.

Then she laid me down on the wicker couch and showed us how she'd arranged her body against his and the motions she'd made with her hands and the different ways she'd tried using her tongue and lips. We were like this—unabashed in our sharing of information and desire to fully understand each other's experiences. The privacy of other people didn't matter. No claim to fidelity could be higher than our own on each other. We didn't have to ask Margaret to demonstrate or prompt her to be thorough and specific. She did things at least half for the opportunity of regaling us with them. She knew we'd want to know.

And did I want to know because I thought this specific information applied to me? Well, I wasn't sure. The summer before, when we were fourteen, my mom had opened the door on me and Margaret sitting on the carpet in my room. It was a million degrees outside. We were entirely naked and taking turns showing each other dumb videos on my laptop. She just shut the door again. Later, she asked if I liked Margaret as more than a friend. I said no, I didn't. She said okay. Though she misread the situation, it would eventually become clear she hadn't misread me.

That was the summer when I first discovered Ginevra, a fairy from a pornographic blog account I read obsessively on my laptop in bed, where I could attempt to resolve any pressing physical urges as they arose by straddling my locked arms or a pillow. Ginevra floated around in a flower city, making out with people. I knew at least that my love for Ginevra did not at all depend on the identity of the person invited to join her within the enormous lilac tree that grew through the center of her verdant cosmopolis.

Eleanor drummed her fingers on the arm of the couch, paying an intense kind of attention to the two of us. She of course wanted to know how to give head because she always wanted to know everything, but she also watched Margaret's bobbing with a look on her face, the high planes of which were pink with creeping rosacea. Behavior of this kind amused and occasionally alarmed her. She wouldn't shower with us. She always said she wanted to shower alone. She scratched her cheeks with her rhinestone nails.

"Be nice to yourself, Eleanor," I said, and she looked away from me, but she lowered her fingers from her face.

Margaret's hand continued to stroke the air between her open mouth and my pelvis until we heard the garage door open and the sound of a car engine turning off. Margaret stumbled away from me and we all started laughing. Eleanor got up to go to the bathroom. The house door to the garage groaned open, and the alarm system beeped in acknowledgment.

"Out back," Margaret called.

A minute later, her mother, Nancy, appeared in the internal doorway of the porch, her blazer slung over one arm, her cellphone between her ear and her shoulder. She'd been on the phone more or less continuously since Margaret's dad had moved out a year ago. She waved to us silently and then retreated into the house to finish her conversation. I loved that Margaret's mom accepted our presence without question. She didn't apologize for being on the phone or hang up to offer us a glass of water and a snack, the way my own mother always did, treating my friends as her guests and trying to attend to them.

We talked for the rest of the afternoon. The sky opened, and rain fell sloppily onto the roof of the porch. Droplets of water clung to the metal grid of its mesh walls in patches, making the green world of the backyard appear blurred, almost pixelated. I asked my friends if I should ask my mom if they could sleep over that night, but Eleanor said she wanted to go home and play *The Sims* for nine hours instead.

She'd stopped playing that morning only because she'd wanted to hang out with us, and now that she had, she wanted to go home and play again. She was in the middle of getting her Sim to sleep with every single one of her in-game neighbors. The plan was proceeding pretty well, except one of her Sim's lovers kept showing up in the middle of the night and letting herself into Eleanor's Sim's house to use the bathroom and watch TV and refuse to leave until morning, when the Sim would spin around in a circle to change her outfit and then depart for work, before inevitably returning the next night to cause the same problem all over again. Eventually, El decided to just drown the interloper in the pool.

Margaret couldn't come over either. She had a family dinner at her aunt and uncle's house with her mom and her cousin Bea and wasn't allowed to make any plans for after. I pouted, but I'd probably see them both the next day anyway.

After several hours of almost tropical intensity, the rain thinned to a mist. The sounds of birds and insects returned. Nancy reappeared to ask if we needed rides home, but Eleanor had her bike and I said I would walk. I texted my mom I was on my way and kissed Margaret on the cheek. I kissed Eleanor on the cheek. I walked the several blocks back to my house beneath rows of dripping trees. Pink and brown earthworms wriggled their naked bodies across the slick, wet sidewalk. If I stepped on any of them, I'd never forgive myself.

THE NEXT MORNING, I WOKE UP LATE TO ABUNDANT SUNSHINE. Light speared through my bedroom windows, forming crisp, elongated rectangles on my bedspread. I made a series of full-body yawns, like a stretching cat. Then I picked up my phone and began to move through the internet.

Eleanor appeared at the top of my feed. She'd posted a photo of herself, half-seated on her bathroom counter in a pair of jeans that gapped from her waist, her back to the mirror and her torso twisted to look over her shoulder. Her white-blond hair framed her face, which was partially obscured by the rectangle of her phone, the lens of its camera hovering in front of her right eye. The slightly upward tilt of her chin directed the bathroom light to fall cleanly on top of her cheekbones, throwing the contours beneath them into flattering shadow. Her heart-shaped face looked rounder in life. The image was like a vision of the future, her child's softness falling away and the dramatic truth of her bone structure rising to the surface. I looked at the picture for a long time. I spread my fingers across the screen to zoom in on the gap between her jeans and her waist. She'd bought the too large pants from the secondhand clothing store we sometimes went to together for this effect, for the sake of taking this kind of photo. If she'd tried to wear them in real life, they would have fallen off. I liked it. I commented with flames. A few seconds later she liked my comment.

I was aware that I greatly enjoyed looking at Eleanor, but the nature of that looking was then still obscure to me. I took pride in her beauty, Margaret's too. I took pride in my own appearance, whenever and for as long as I could manage it. I had been known to stand in front of a mirror and make a variety of faces. I took a screenshot of the post and then a minute later deleted it. I could always come back and look through her profile if I wanted to.

I kept scrolling: a *Sailor Moon* meme; a pristine purse on a shoulder; a friend from school, pores blurred to within an inch of her life; and then a chain of girls from the grade above us posting photos of ice cream cones. None of them had shared the whole group together. Instead, there was a sequence of hands and ankles in the backgrounds of images, a chorus of laughter overheard on a video, the fact that all the ice cream cones had come from the same place and that all the images were taken at the same time of day. In other words, there was a sufficient accumulation of information to declare that a group of girls had all been together without any of them having to say so. None of them were tagged. They knew it wasn't necessary.

I kept looking, my thumb alternately tapping forward and holding videos in place. I could tell that, at some point, some of the girls had gone home, probably because their mothers made them. The rest continued posting into the evening. The lighting dropped to night. Then the girls themselves began to appear in the pictures, standing on the train tracks that cut through our neighborhood. They hadn't actually gotten on the train. Whether or not they would have been allowed to go anywhere, they didn't in fact have anywhere to go. The transit line led to office parks and eventually the hospital. Rather, the infrastructure served as a destination in itself. Any non-domestic location, any place that could be gotten to without a car and that didn't belong to a family, had value as a setting.

I flipped through a series of brightly illuminated flash photos of the girls posing against the tracks. They wore sweatpants and sweatshirts, but their hair was straightened and then curled, and their black eyeliner made their eyes large and visible. Finally, at the end of the night, they wound up at the playground of the lower school near my house. There they met two other girls who I could see in the background of a video. One of them had on a cool jean jacket—I recognized her—and the other one was Margaret.

In such circumstances, I typically called Eleanor—the only person to whom I was willing to complain. After two rings, Eleanor's face bloomed into my screen. Every time I video-chatted her, she was walking from one place to another. Her face slid back and forth across the rectangle in my hand, trees shifting behind her head in rhythm with her step. From the way she glanced down at me through the screen, I knew she'd seen the video of Margaret.

"I can come over at three," she said.

I invited Margaret too, but she didn't text me back.

In the meantime, I felt obligated to pick a fight with my mother. Actually she picked the fight with me, but I lacked the restraint to decline. We were sitting on the couch. She gestured at my yesterday's curled-up socks on the ground.

"The key is to put things away as you use them," she said.

She was always coming up with keys.

"Then you're continually cleaning up instead of just sometimes," I said.

"No, then you never really have to clean up because it's already mostly done."

I tucked my legs underneath myself, depressing the cushion. "I'm not talking about housekeeping right now," I protested. I'd been telling her I wanted Eleanor to come over.

"I'm just saying," she went on. "We could both do better."

I couldn't fathom her determination to irritate me over something as unimportant as socks. She had terrible priorities. I hated her priorities.

"You always turn what I'm talking about into something else that I'm not talking about. That's not how people have conversations." A wary look entered her face, which only inflamed me further. "Stop telling me what to do for like five seconds," I said.

"Okay, Mina, okay." She stood up.

"Where are you going?" I was mad at her, but I hadn't released her. Of the two of us, I thought, only I should have the right to leave a conversation.

"To get some water from the kitchen," she said.

One benefit of mothers is the permanent availability of a person with whom to disagree. Margaret, on the other hand, I wasn't yet really within my rights to upbraid. Yes, she'd said she couldn't hang out on account of family plans, but then she'd been with Bea, and Bea was family, Bea's mom being Margaret's mom's sister. And I never could have gone with her anyway. I wouldn't have been allowed to go, and I didn't sneak out. Which meant Margaret should have told me. She shouldn't have made me find something out about her from the internet. Still, even I, who considered friendship an ethical undertaking, couldn't be mad at Margaret for not having told me something that happened only six hours ago.

I would have liked to confide in my mother because then she would have comforted me, but I couldn't in any way reveal that Margaret had hurt me, even if the hurt was slight and temporary, because then I'd have to come back later and convince her that everything was okay, and some part of her wouldn't believe in the reconciliation. She never forgot anyone who had ever wronged me.

I also couldn't explain what I'd seen without alarming her. If I made it seem like Margaret participated in compromising or forbidden situations, situations in which I could at some point become embroiled, then she might not let me sleep over at Margaret's house as often as she did, which was already less often than both Eleanor and Margaret were allowed to sleep at each other's houses or my house, and I didn't want that. Not that she would ever meaningfully separate me from Margaret by her own standards—we'd been best friends since kindergarten, she loved Margaret—but she might by mine. She was mystified by the intensity of my feelings in general but especially by the ferocity of my friendships, what I needed from them, how I twined my life around them.

Why did I want to have so many sleepovers? my mom sometimes asked. Why couldn't I just hang out and then come home to rest in my own bed? What was so important about being unconscious next to someone who you were going to see the next day anyway? I thought these questions were a trick—she wanted me to admit that we stayed up all night carousing. It's true she underestimated the quantity of togetherness lost by going home after dinner instead of the next morning, but even if we did go straight to bed, it seemed obvious to me that sleeping next to someone was an act of intimacy unavailable during regular visiting hours: to wear your pajamas and wash your face above the sink, to watch a girl's eyes flutter closed. Both my friends, at least, understood this.

When my mom returned from the kitchen, she brought me a glass. I took it.

At three, El glided into my driveway on her bike, standing on its pedals. She wore a green pleated tennis dress and no helmet. Her pale-blond hair licked her temples in the humidity, the air of the afternoon lousy with thoughts of rain. She hugged me briefly.

"I haven't showered," she said. She'd come straight here from practice.

"It's fine," I answered. "You always smell good."

I led us inside, where we first said hello to my mother, who expected anyone who entered her house to spend at least one minute acknowledging her existence. She'd told me so repeatedly, that I couldn't just slink upstairs with a friend. We found her sitting on the far side of the dinner table, slicing through mail with a kitchen knife. Even seated, she looked tall, her brown and silver hair in a braid down her back, lighter in color than my own, my dark features having come from my father, who was also tall and who made most of his appearances after dark and over the weekend.

"How's your mom?" my mom asked Eleanor, setting aside an envelope.

She saved the preprinted return-address labels sent to her by nonprofit organizations seeking donations if they had birds or flowers on them. She threw away the ones with American flags or frogs because she didn't like looking at frogs or nationalism as a marketing strategy.

"She abandoned me for Chicago," Eleanor said, which meant her mom had gone away on a brief trip for work.

"You're welcome to stay for dinner," my mom offered.

"Then who will eat all my cereal?" Eleanor asked.

She was a real expert at finding ways to say no to people. Also, she loved eating cereal for dinner. I knew Eleanor saw the differences between my relationship with my mom and her relationship with hers, but I couldn't yet imagine that she might resent her mother's occasional absences in the same way I resented my mother's continuous presence.

We climbed the stairs to my bedroom.

I had a queen-sized bed, a desk, two wide windows with wood-slat blinds, and a very big mirror on the opposite wall. I had an orchid on its fifth bloom, which my mother watered weekly by placing an ice cube on top of its soil, the only times I voluntarily invited her into my room. I suspected she used the opportunity to surreptitiously collect laundry. Pajamas and sweaters mounded on my desk chair. On my bedside table sat a lamp with a shade shaped like a cloud and above my bed hung a framed illustration of a pink winged chalice.

"Show me your people," Eleanor said, which was what we called playing *The Sims*. Playing *The Sims* was one of the things Eleanor and I did together when we hung out just the two of us. I pulled my lavender bedsheet up from its rumple at the foot of the bed to cover the mattress. Then I pulled my duvet over the sheet and arranged my four pillows into a headboard for the both of us, and we sat on top of the frothy covers. All my windows were pushed up. The plants outside shook against one another like instruments in the pre-rain wind. June in Ohio was always either wet or promising to be.

I launched the game on my laptop. A large, multifaceted green diamond spun in the center of the screen while loading messages played: *When the reaper appears on the whispering wishing well, you wish at your own peril.*

The game loaded an overhead view of my basic neighborhood of houses. I selected the one in which my Sim lived, a tiny rectangle on a large empty lot. Another load screen appeared. Eleanor began to braid a piece of her hair. She pulled her legs up beside her. She didn't shave them, which I would have considered an almost miraculous act of rebellion except that the hair on Eleanor's legs, like the hair on the rest of her body, was so white-blond, it nearly disappeared against her skin. I fanned my fingers over my keyboard without depressing any of the keys for the sake of the satisfying sound it produced.

"Mar probably knows we know," I said.

"Probably," she responded, and tilted her head to one side to get a better look at her hair. "But Mar is always willing to act like she's gotten away with something until it's been proven to her that she hasn't."

I nodded. This was an accurate description of Margaret's relationship with her mother. I just didn't want it to also be how she was treating us. Everything that had to do with my friends was my business. I couldn't imagine why Margaret hadn't already told us something of such obvious interest. The green diamond continued to spin.

"She still might tell us," Eleanor said.

I picked up a clear plastic hair tie from my bedside table. Instead of handing it to her, I took Eleanor's pale braid from between her fingers and tied it off myself, the miniature plaits she'd made perfectly even.

"Do mine please," I said, and separated a section of hair from the right side of my face, which she wordlessly took.

She had to rise up onto her knees to reach the top of my head. Her chest touched my shoulder. She separated my hair into strands and began to braid, her hold firm and her fingers quick, the sensation familiar. Every time I saw El braiding her hair, I asked her to braid mine.

I went on, "But if Mar isn't deliberately keeping it a secret, wouldn't she have already posted?"

Margaret could be counted on to post evidence, however oblique, whenever she did anything fun. The more fun, the more oblique. The image had to be explicable to her mother under duress, if it came to that. Of our three moms, only Nancy attempted to keep track of her daughter's social media use. My mom believed in the value of privacy, perhaps as a counterweight to her insistence on total honesty and disclosure. Also, she had no social media of her own and therefore lacked a means of looking.

"Maybe she thinks it's fun to have done something we don't immediately know about," Eleanor suggested.

The next screen loaded, but I paused the game so we could keep talking.

I loved talking to Eleanor like this, privately investigating a topic at hand, with the air full of rain. If and when Margaret hurt me, at least I got to talk to Eleanor about it.

"That doesn't bother you?" I asked.

"I mean," she said. "Neither of you ever tells me everything."

The words weren't sharp, but I'd never heard them from her before. As a matter of policy between the three of us, we didn't verbalize my and Margaret's closer tie, the inimitable result of a lifetime of friendship. I realized in my eagerness I'd maybe pushed Eleanor into a painful admission and felt ashamed.

I didn't know how to ask for forgiveness, however, so instead I looked at my computer screen, where my Sim and her tiny rectangular house were waiting.

"I'm not spending any money on furniture yet," I explained.

I had increased the difficulty of the game by artificially wasting almost all of my Sim's starter cash on a set of expensive symbolic objects, which I kept in her inventory where they couldn't positively affect her mood. I also refused to use cheat codes, which were an accepted standard of play among the fan base, because I thought they made the game lose its purpose and texture. Why make my Sim do anything if I could solve their every problem with a phrase?

Eleanor found all this very funny behavior on my part because she treated her Sims as unholy social experiments and exploited every loophole in the game. When played according to its base premise and on good-faith terms, *The Sims* was too easy. You'd get bored in a few hours. Which was why so many people played the game like Eleanor, in pursuit of extremity, or like me, in pursuit of achievement. Regardless of these differences in gameplay philosophy, we both cared the most about our Sims' quest for relationships. You could get a lot done riding on the mood boosts provided by romantic interactions. You could get your Sim to do all sorts of unpleasant things if their mood was full pink from smooching.

"Ginevra?" Eleanor asked when she saw my character's name in the upper-left-hand corner of the screen.

"Haha, yeah," I said. "I thought it was a funny name."

She didn't question me further, and I didn't explain. Her Sims also had suspicious names like Bella Goth the XIV and Dumb Slut of the greater Slut family and Sally Dalloway.

Ginevra had lilac hair and amazing boobs—boobs I had manually adjusted to be not quite but nearly as large as the mechanisms of the game allowed. This token act of restraint assuaged some of my embarrassment about making a body to play with. I liked watching her run on the treadmill at the gym. I thought if I named a Sim after Ginevra the fairy, then she ought to at least have some evidence of physical prowess. Also I gave her a trait that made her happy every time she went outside.

"She's a vibe," Eleanor said. "Should we get her pregnant?"

"I'm not ready yet," I answered. "I'm not done with her career.

She still needs to play a lot more chess before she's ready to have a baby, okay?"

Playing chess helped fulfill the game requirements for promotion in Ginevra's career track as a *Scientist*.

"Okay, I won't demand we light anyone on fire," Eleanor countered. "But can we please at least tell Ginevra to go sex a member of the community?"

I agreed that was reasonable. The next question was who. Rather than taking the time to make an attractive Sim from scratch and introduce them to Ginevra, we chose a game-generated citizen of the township with whom she had already established a relationship.

"They're *Very Good Friends,* but I haven't started flirting with him yet," I said. Meaning I had only used interactions from the *Friendly* social menu and none from the *Romantic* one.

"He has a goatee," Eleanor said.

"That's true but would not affect their future babies."

Eleanor graciously skipped pointing out that I'd changed my mind with respect to impregnating my Sim. Having finished my braid, she resumed her seat by my side, her knee against mine. We had to sit close together in order to both see the screen. My laptop, always warm, began to truly overheat. It was an old computer, and the game taxed its systems. After every fifteen minutes or so of gameplay, its internal fan would reach an alarming hum, and I'd have to hold the laptop out in the air above me like a baby in order to cool it down.

My laptop back on my lap, Ginevra used her cellphone to invite Gavin Richards to the park in her in-game neighborhood. She would be more amenable to flirtation in an outdoor setting. The two Sims materialized at the edge of the lot. I paused before Ginevra and Gavin could begin self-generating behavior. While playing the game, you had control over only the characters in your household, but if you assigned actions to your Sim that implicated someone outside your household, the game would make the other Sim available to participate.

I assigned Ginevra a queue of actions from the *Friendly* menu. If you used interactions from the *Romantic* menu too quickly, the other Sim got weirded out, which then made your Sim feel embarrassed. I un-paused the game. Ginevra and Gavin began to address each other with animated gibberish. Ginevra produced a speech bubble with an image of a rainbow in it. Gavin replied with an image of a slice of pizza.

"Have her *Tell a Flirtatious Joke,*" Eleanor said.

"It's too soon," I countered. "Give it a minute."

"Have them take off all their clothes and run around the park naked."

Interestingly, streaking had no effect on the Sims' relationship with each other and relied on a threshold of *Friendliness* rather than *Romance* to activate. Streaking together was apparently considered by the game purely amicable, and therefore we didn't have time for it.

"Lol but no," I said. "We can't waste their good need bars if we want them to hook up before they have to go home and sleep."

"Just buff their moods, so we can play with them for longer."

Ignoring this suggestion, I paused the game again to add a string of *Romantic* actions to the queue. We were playing at my house on my save file, so I got to make the decisions. Pink plus signs began to appear above their heads as Ginevra successfully *Confessed Her Attraction,* but when she tried to *Give a Massage,* Gavin shook his head and Ginevra stepped away looking ashamed. The game added a yellow embarrassed effect to her mood status. I quickly canceled my planned escalation of interactions and added back in some lower-stakes gestures. I told her to *Compliment Appearance,* and he fanned his face as though overwhelmed. A few minutes later, they successfully executed their first kiss. Congratulatory music played. Their moods both turned very pink and flirty.

Maybe I was glad that Margaret hadn't texted me back and that Eleanor had come over by herself to talk to me, because I felt alarmed by Margaret's adventure in the mall parking lot. I felt like I was eighty years away from having oral sex with anyone. I felt like by the time we went to college Margaret would be an adult woman, and I would be a frog wearing a bow on its head. I had been kissed fewer than five total times in my life, and none of them really counted. I thought a kiss only counted if you liked it a lot. Margaret counted all her kisses, including the ones she didn't like. Eleanor counted all her kisses too, but she never actually described them to me, so they felt less real.

"Should we make them get married?" she asked.

"No way," I said, but then felt shy about my vehemence. "Ginevra has high standards."

"You're right," Eleanor agreed. "If she gets married, then you won't let her *WooHoo* with anyone else. Now make them *Kiss Passionately*."

I did what she said.

"Have them do it again."

They did it again.

I turned to face Eleanor for her reaction, but she was already looking at me. I thought one of us should laugh, but neither of us did. We looked back at the computer screen.

"I don't want them to get married, because I don't want him to move into her household," I explained. El nodded but said nothing. I opened the *Romantic* menu again and saw that the options we'd been waiting for were now available to us.

"You might as well *Try for Baby,*" she said. "Like as long as we're here."

I didn't argue. I'd rather get Ginevra pregnant with Eleanor than by myself. In fact, I wondered if there were any other Sims I could impregnate while Eleanor was still with me. I wondered how close I should zoom in the view of the game to watch what happened next. Only somewhat, I decided. Too close and the game lost its overhead perspective.

Try for Baby automatically made use of the nearest eligible object, usually a bed or a shower or a walk-in closet, but because Ginevra and Gavin were at the park, they walked single file in synchronized step to a large bush with red flowers at the perimeter of the lot. They stood in front of the bush, turned simultaneously to face each other, and then leapt into its foliage. The bush began to quiver, shimmy, shiver. It emitted delighted Sim sounds and steam animations until eventually the whole plant jumped in climax, and tiny fireworks erupted above its leaves. At last, the two Sims emerged looking smuttily pleased with themselves and straightened their clothing.

Try for Baby had a high but not quite guaranteed success rate, so we felt justified in instructing Ginevra and Gavin to repeat the action six or seven times to be sure it had worked. By the end of their marathon, most of Ginevra's need bars were deeply red from neglect, but her social bar was a pulsing lime-green rod. I sent Ginevra back to her house alone to go to the bathroom, eat leftover grilled cheese, take a shower, and go to bed. Twenty-four hours of game time later, we got a notification that she was pregnant.

"We should brag to Margaret," I said. "She may have gone

down on a live human boy, but we collectively impregnated a tiny digital woman."

Eleanor rolled her gray eyes at me. "Text me a picture when the baby's born," she said. She had to go home. "I want to know if it inherits her purple hair."

After she left, I put my laptop on the ground next to my bed. The computer was too hot from the game. I wanted to keep playing but I needed to touch myself first. Ginevra sometimes had that effect on me.

BY FRIDAY, I WAS BACK AT MARGARET'S HOUSE WITH AN ITCHINESS between us. I found her to be too pleased with herself. She flitted around her room with authority and half an eye on her phone at all times.

"Don't ask me what we're doing tonight," Margaret said. "I'm serious. Don't even look at me with that face. It's too early for discussion."

She maintained an almost superstitious attitude about social plans while she was in the process of seeking them out. She wanted our silent and appreciative awareness of her efforts without any questions or comments on her progress. To speak an intention was to limit the luminous sensation of possibility. In tank tops and underwear, we crossed the wood floor of Margaret's bedroom to the tile in her bathroom and back again, moving between our clothes and our makeup.

"How's Starter Penis?" I asked instead.

"We've been talking," she said, drawing out the word *talking*.

She pulled up their text thread on her phone and scanned through their recent messages, so I could see the frequency of communication between them, but with quick enough strokes that I couldn't read what either of them had said.

"What do you talk about?" I asked. I had hardly flirted with anybody in my life. I had no idea what you texted someone you wanted to hook up with. "Like what do you say?"

"Honestly, it's vague," Margaret said. "It's ambiently horny."

She thought he might invite us somewhere that night. I could tell she was convinced he would. She gestured at one of the seven complete outfits I'd brought to her house and dispersed onto her floor for our mutual perusal, and I tried it on. A black halter top with flower-shaped cutouts on either side of my waist and matching skirt.

"Oh my God," she said when I walked into the doorway that connected her bedroom to her bathroom. Hair tools, Q-tips, tubes of mascara, eyeliner pencil stubs, and open eyeshadow palettes leaking colorful dust covered every available surface. "You look so hot."

I raised my arm into the air in answer and let my fingertips graze the doorframe. My hair, which reached beyond my ribs, skimmed the skin of my waist exposed by the cutouts.

"Thank you," I said.

I thought she was about to tell me about Wednesday night unprompted now that we were in person and alone together, but she didn't. She just applied primer to her cheeks and forehead and waved her hands in front of her face to dry the product.

To my envy, Margaret lived in the attic of her house, with her own bedroom and bathroom and an ancient storage closet in which we'd once found old journals belonging to Margaret's mother. I refused to read them, so Margaret read them and gave me quotes and summaries until she decided she didn't want to read them either, and we put them away. Margaret's attic, though blessedly private, was also hot in the summer, the best efforts of its in-window air conditioner insufficient for the heat that had been seeping upward all afternoon. We walked back to the bedroom to stand in front of the enormous industrial fan at its center. The fan whipped our hair from our cheeks and necks. I took off my halter top outfit, but instead of immediately trying on one of the alternatives lying on the floor, I stood there with Margaret, talking in our underwear, trying not to sweat. Half an hour later, Eleanor arrived.

We watched her climb the stairs to the attic two at a time. She held a small, monogrammed tote bag beneath her shoulder and a metal water bottle like a missile in her hand, ice cubes jostling within as she climbed. Her platform sandals made her tall, though still not as tall as I was. She hugged me first. Our ears touched.

"So what are we doing after dinner?" Eleanor immediately asked Margaret with a sly look of provocation on her face.

My eyes rimmed hers.

"We're throwing an orgy," I said before Margaret could sour. "We're defending the planet against an invasive force of hot acrobats wearing leotards and large ruffled collars," a reference to *Sailor Moon.*

"Fun," Eleanor replied, and let it drop.

She walked in front of me into the bathroom, where music played from Margaret's phone. We'd set the phone into a glass cup from the kitchen to amplify its sound, so the emphatic bass line pulsed in the confined space, its beats overlaid with women's voices singing in ethereal tones. Eleanor sat down on the closed lid of the toilet, lifted the phone from the cup, and, without anyone's permission, began to edit the queue of songs.

Margaret resumed her makeup routine using her mother's products, which she couldn't share with us because she wasn't supposed to be using them in the first place. I plugged my straightener into the wall outlet next to the sink and began to section my hair. She tapped concealer onto her various blemishes, careful not to thin the product in its application. I ran a brush across my scalp for the sensation of its bristles' rake. My hair's natural wave expanded with static. She started fanning her face again to set the layer. I passed the wand slowly down the length of a section and observed the strands' silken realignment. I didn't wish I had straight hair, because then I would've missed out on the pleasure of straightening it.

Eleanor returned Margaret's phone to the glass cup. She required less time for assembly than the two of us because in place of wearing much makeup, she maintained a complex and multilayered skincare routine. She pressed all her serums into her face by herself before she came over. Her skin looked dewy and reflective. I'd seen the process many times when I slept at her house. I'd watched her fingertips sink into her cheeks. Once, I told her she could bring her skincare with her like we brought our makeup, but she refused on the basis that then she'd have to use someone else's towel. Still, she wouldn't miss getting ready together as an event.

What we loved was to feel attractive in each other's company, to spur each other on to greater beauty and to experience this ascension as a series of steps we could teach each other to perform—first bronzer, then contour, then a smudged and smoky eyeliner. We complimented each other as we worked, and we accepted all of each other's compliments without the reserve or suspicion that usually results from a person commenting upon your appearance. Whatever my friends said about me, I believed them.

Margaret's phone dinged in its cup. She turned from the mirror immediately and picked it up. She grazed the message with her eyes, testing for its tenor, and then looked away. She glanced at herself in the mirror, flicked her hair once, and then returned her phone to the cup without typing anything back. She was disappointed. I saw her note the time on the lock screen and wondered how long she'd determined to wait before replying.

I picked up a fluffy makeup brush from my zippered bag and began dusting bronzer in between my boobs, at first haphazardly, then with greater precision, running the brush along the curve of the left and then the curve of the right to exaggerate their shadows. Then I picked up a smaller brush, coated it in a pearlescent highlighter, and tapped the shimmering powder onto the tops of each. Margaret, who had begun to apply further coats of mascara, paused with her mouth open to watch what I was doing in the mirror.

Though I consciously restrained my gaze to the foreground of the reflection, where Margaret and I stood by the sink, I felt Eleanor's presence both behind and in front of me as I moved the brush up and down my chest. I knew she regarded my movements through the mirror from her seat. I also knew I couldn't look at her if I wanted her to continue looking at me.

"Wait," Margaret said, admiration obvious in her voice. "Are you contouring your boobs right now?"

The question broke Eleanor's gaze. I felt its withdrawal and followed. She lifted Margaret's phone and scrolled in a rote manner through the list of songs on the screen. Then without apparently adding any of them to the queue, she put the phone down again. I nodded.

"Okay, she's a genius," Margaret announced, so I felt like a genius. "Do mine?"

I gave a baby dramatic roll of the eyes and smiled when I said, "Of course."

Margaret was right about the reasonableness of her plan superstition, at least in the sense that we didn't actually need to know where we were going or what we were doing that night in order to get dressed. It was summer. It was Friday. We would ready ourselves into a state of hotness sufficient for whatever the universe might be so good as to offer us. Unspoken but also agreed upon, we would ready ourselves into a state of hotness usable by Margaret in getting this boy to hang out with her. Presumably, he also had friends.

I enjoyed being considered eligible for this service more than I enjoyed performing it. Given the choice between hanging out with exclusively Margaret and Eleanor and hanging out with Margaret and Eleanor plus other people, I almost always would have chosen to spend my time as just the three of us. And I hated having to ask my mother for additional permissions in real time with my friends waiting to find out whether or not my presence was about to become a problem. Whenever my mom said no to me, my organs melted in my stomach. Also, I didn't care very much about hanging out with boys.

Margaret left and came back in a new bra, the straps of which could be hooked together into an X across her back to draw her boobs toward the center of her chest. Then she reached into each cup and moved her flesh up and forward, so that her nipples were all the way at the edges of the fabric. I could see the pink rims of her areolas folding over the lace of the bra. The effect provided as much cleavage as she could, at that time, possibly have had. I stepped back and bent over slightly, Margaret being a few inches shorter than I was, to repeat the process on her chest, dragging the bronzer brush along the center of each curve and tapping the highlighter brush along the tops.

"You are both deeply extra," Eleanor said.

A thread of exasperation had entered her voice.

I felt the moment arrive, the moment most optimal for

Margaret to spontaneously reveal she'd snuck out with Bea. Eleanor and I were both present, and Margaret was in the midst of not getting exactly what she wanted from the boy she was texting. As the seconds passed, I realized she wasn't going to take the opportunity. She wasn't going to say anything. And I realized Eleanor had seen all this occur to me because she'd observed the same. Which meant that if I didn't ask my best friend now, at the last instant before what she hadn't told us could become a secret she'd genuinely withheld, then I was a coward, and I couldn't stand to be a coward in front of Eleanor, who hated cowardice, so I asked defiantly, "How was Wednesday night?"

Margaret took her time to reply. She pushed her chestnut hair over her shoulder and leaned toward the mirror to insert a small stud earring in the shape of a butterfly through the hole in her right ear. Then she told the story easily, without embarrassment, without accounting for not having told it already, and without inquiring how I'd known to ask.

She and Bea had continued hanging out after their shared family dinner. Bea had a car and could drive them wherever they could find to go. They went to a late movie, the two of them. Their mothers assented because anything the cousins did together could be considered family time. Then they continued on to the playground, where they saw a mixture of people from our grade and Bea's.

"Olivia was like fully drunk," she said, Olivia being Bea's best friend. "She kept trying to get people to sit down on the ground with her."

"As one does," I said, as though I had any idea.

I'd made the three of us all promise we'd get drunk for the first time together, just us. Not because I worried about missing out on some specific invitation but rather because I feared the effect of cumulative divergent experience. I didn't want my friends to turn into other people without me.

"Olivia is suspicious," Eleanor responded, "because she posts group photos in which she's only edited her own face. Or like max, also Bea's face. Why does she think no one will notice? Though she's very good at blow-drying her hair."

I agreed. I liked Bea and Olivia, and also they annoyed me. Margaret's phone illuminated again. She whirled to lift it, but didn't respond to this message either. When her eyes returned to ours, she pointed at Eleanor.

"Get your bag," she said. "I want to see what you're wearing."

The monogram on the bag read BYE. Inside, a couple of neatly folded items of clothing. Eleanor only ever brought one outfit.

THE HOSTESS LED US THROUGH THE CROWDED RESTAURANT, PASSing red booth tables and people with pizza in their mouths, all of them families, kids seated on laps and leaning from raised chairs, men wearing sports paraphernalia, and women with unwashed hair. Figuratively, we were overdressed. I'd stuck rhinestones to the corners of El's gray eyes. Literally, we were underdressed, our clothing covering only a very limited portion of our bodies. I gripped my phone tightly in my right hand. I hadn't brought a purse, because I thought purses were stupid; I had nothing to put in one. We'd known what the scene would be at the restaurant—we'd all eaten there a hundred times—but chosen to pursue our outfits anyway.

We didn't mind. Well, we meant not to mind. But now that we'd arrived, I felt pretty conspicuous, pretty dramatically out of sorts with our environment, the artistry I'd performed on my own and Margaret's chests too visible beneath the fluorescent lights. These weren't the people I wanted to look at my boobs. I couldn't have said who were—an uncertainty that fed my love of posting photos. One benefit of the internet is the generalized audience for your body. My height didn't help either. I was almost five foot eight at the time, with coltish legs and a wingspan half a size too large for my body. I knew I sometimes startled women in the grocery store with my baby face appearing so high up in the air. I was aware or wanted to believe that my height was an advantage.

Models were tall. Girls on the internet were tall or positioned their cameras so as to appear to be. Boys I didn't like found my size discouraging. Still, at times like this, I wished the process would slow down a little. I had years left in which to eventually match my mother's even six feet.

At the same time, I felt protected by the banal familiarity of the restaurant. This wasn't really the grand swimming pool of the world, just a puddle in which we were free to titillate ourselves by splashing around half naked. And if we looked nothing akin to anyone else, we looked entirely right with each other, Eleanor in her hot-pink linen matching set cropped camisole and high-rise A-line miniskirt and me and Margaret in the related but unidentical dresses we'd eventually chosen to reveal our contoured chests. I tried to settle into the silk skin of our cumulative effect. I may have made what hips I had swish. If you feel like disappearing, sometimes the best countermeasure is to make yourself more visible.

Margaret waved to a friend of her mother's, whose husband was wearing cargo shorts and a pair of water sandals. Ohio will not allow you to pretend you're anywhere else. She walked over to greet them, abandoning me and Eleanor to follow the hostess. Eleanor slid into the booth across from me, our eyes on each other in acknowledgment of the miniature social predicaments into which Margaret so often thrust us and herself. Absently, she raised a hand to her face.

"They're still there," I said of the rhinestones. She looked embarrassed instead of relieved.

Margaret returned to us with a report. Some girl we sort of knew had been forced to come home from camp early on account of an untreated urinary tract infection that turned into a kidney infection for which she'd had to go to the hospital. We ordered our pizza and settled in to discuss.

"Obviously she was having a lot of sex at camp and didn't know you're supposed to pee afterward," Margaret said, scooting farther into the booth beside me.

We knew you were supposed to pee afterward because one of Eleanor's older sisters had told her and she'd told us, and now Margaret acted as though this were information she'd had all along.

"You're insane," Eleanor said. "I don't know how you get people to tell you these things in like the briefest interactions."

Margaret preened.

"It's an effect she has," I explained. "She pulls the gossip out of people with her face." I took Margaret's cheeks into my hands, looked into her eyes, and said in a hypnotized voice, "I must reveal all my secrets."

"Yes, tell me," Margaret said.

I let go of her face and shrugged. "You know them all already."

Eleanor, who had wedged her hands palms down beneath her thighs, leaned forward onto the table conspiratorially.

"What about my face?" she asked. "What does my face tell you to do?"

Anxiety fluttered like fabric in the breeze of my mind, the sense that I needed to perform—or risk loss. El never would have asked anyone else to tell her who she was.

"Your face says you already know everything, and so you don't need to be told."

She gave me a fae grin of satisfaction. I received it as a physical reward, the hair on my arms all gone upright. This was, at the time, how I saw Eleanor and how she herself most wanted to be seen—complete, already in possession of whatever it was most people sought from each other—neither of us yet realizing what this impression might serve to conceal.

Our waitress walked by with somebody else's pizza over her shoulder.

Margaret flipped her phone over. She'd been keeping it face down on the table. We all saw her lock screen light up, a picture of the three of us, without any new notifications. She turned it over again. By then, it was clear we had no plan. I thought probably no plan would present itself. No one we knew was about to unexpectedly throw a party. No friends of ours had access to vacant houses or knew doormen at bars who accepted drastically underaged patrons. There weren't even any bars nearby, just restaurants with seats and alcohol. Not that eons of teenagers in our neighborhood hadn't previously overcome these limitations in the name of debauchery. I just didn't think we were capable of joining them, not yet.

Condensation from our red plastic tumblers of ice water pooled on the almost laminated surface of the table. Eleanor touched the torn white paper wrapper from her straw just barely to the lip of the water. Liquid climbed and dampened the paper. The wait for food dragged. We found ourselves neither on the way to nor from an experience, so we could neither anticipate future fanfare nor retroactively assign significance to the medium amount of fun we'd already had. We just had to sit there and wait for pizza in a restaurant full of babies.

"I'm trying Bea," Margaret announced, so we would know she'd given up on the boy without us having to ask. Probably she'd double-texted him and not heard back. The shame of wanting something from someone who wasn't giving it to her made

Margaret agitated and determined. My nerves prickled in my armpits.

"Worst-case scenario—" I began to suggest, but she pushed back right away.

"No. No worst-case scenario. We're going out. Mandatory."

"Yeah," Eleanor agreed. She never had to say no to anything. She was allowed to go wherever she was invited. "It's mandatory."

When the pizza came, at least we could take pictures of ourselves. Margaret crossed her arms to exaggerate her cleavage and leaned her head on my shoulder while I smiled. I crossed my arms for the same reason and fed a slice of pizza to Margaret, who mimed eating it. Then I switched to the other side of the booth, so that Eleanor wouldn't have to take pictures by herself. I leaned my back up against hers and pouted. She rolled her eyes until they went all the way white beside the rhinestones and stuck out her tongue. Even though we moved through these poses quickly, I couldn't help looking around the restaurant to apologize with my eyes for behaving so conspicuously like denizens of the internet. But I wanted the pictures. I wanted the documentation, the proof of the three of us at every minute. And I conceded to myself that we weren't really doing anything wrong, just making a minor spectacle with our conscious girlness that everybody else was free to ignore.

I never returned to the other side of the table. We paid the check at the front. Each of us put a mint in our mouths.

WE WALKED HOME FROM DINNER INEFFICIENTLY, UNWILLING TO acquiesce to the universe's disinterest in our pleasure. It was such a lusciously golden evening, only a week before the summer solstice, the boundaries of daylight near their loosest of the year. The sun wouldn't set until after nine, the sidewalk still warm to the palm I laid on its dimpled surface to check. Having nothing else to do, we took more pictures of ourselves in the perfect after-dinner light. Sitting, squatting, standing, with the sky as a background, with the grass as a background, with the camera set to self-timer on the hood of someone's car, Margaret on top of a fire hydrant holding on to the stem of a stop sign, Eleanor refusing to lie down on a front yard because she didn't want grass stains, me with my head tipped back and my hair swinging between my shoulder blades.

Shouldn't something happen to us? Shouldn't a star fall on our heads? Hadn't our bodies shaken anything loose from the universe? The pulse of these questions in my chest felt like enough for me. There is safety in longing for what you know you won't get. I didn't want to have to say no to something as always. I didn't want to prevent my friends from scaling a fence or jumping into some house's pool or stealing an orange traffic cone with no plan for where to put it. *Please don't make me,* I thought. *Please, please*—and yet I had my own summer urgency too, the sense that something had to happen to us, and we were wasting time if it didn't, that we couldn't return to school in two months exactly the same as who we'd been when we left it. Eventually, an SUV full of boys we recognized drove by and honked at us, which, we agreed, represented at least some comment from the populace on our efforts.

Bea called Margaret back, and I felt vaguely sick.

When Margaret answered the video chat, Bea said, "Hey, babe," from the passenger seat of a car that evidently wasn't hers.

Bea had naturally auburn hair, which she dyed a deep brown and then straightened too often for the health of its ends. I didn't want to get roped into Bea's night, because I had limited faith in Bea's judgment and no faith at all in Margaret's ability to refuse her older cousin. She held out her phone so the camera included me and Eleanor. We put our arms around her waist and squeezed our cheeks into her cheeks to fit. She mentioned the boys with an eye roll.

"We were like, *Hello, yes, we're walking down the street. Congratulations.*"

Bea laughed and then looked offscreen to provide directions to the unseen driver beside her.

"What are you up to?" Margaret asked, which was as close as she'd come to requesting an invitation. Margaret always tried to approach Bea from even ground, which rarely proved possible because Bea had been born a year before Margaret and hadn't wasted any of her time since. She owned a vibrator I'd seen a picture of and had third piercings, both her ears decked with dangling metal.

Instead of answering, Bea said she had to go because they were about to merge onto the highway and she needed to focus. We circled as many additional blocks as we could reasonably justify and returned to Margaret's house dissatisfied with the uselessness of our good looks. No one else was home. We changed into our pajamas but couldn't stomach the removal of our hair and makeup. I didn't say anything, but Margaret still knew I felt relieved and as a result became irritable with me.

"Mina," she said. "Why didn't you bring back the shorts I lent you?" She was wearing one of my softest sweatshirts when she said this, which she'd taken from my house six months ago without asking.

Eleanor intervened by setting up a playlist of music videos on Margaret's laptop in the living room. We began to dance. We alternated between sexual thrusting and donning blankets like capes to run around in circles with only half-hearted enthusiasm. Nancy called at ten-thirty, and Margaret left the room to answer. She found it easier to finesse her mother without the two of us actively listening.

In her absence, Eleanor and I fell onto the couch, relieved from our duty of merrymaking. The sun had set. The night ran hot and clear. A soft commotion of summer insects sounded through the living room's raised windows. Frogs carried on long-distance conversations. Eleanor picked up a section of her hair and began braiding its strands. She'd sat so close to me on the couch that when she shifted her weight the cushions collapsed between our bodies and our thighs touched knee to hip.

"Mar makes me tired," I whispered. Margaret's resentment of our failure to produce an adequate escalation annoyed me. Us sitting at home on a Friday night marred her emerging narrative of this summer as transformational, as replete with unarticulated potential, as who knew what might happen so long as it wasn't nothing. "Like I'm sorry I'm not a boy she can hook up with to make this night sufficiently legendary," I said. I found her need to make pace exhausting, and I thought Eleanor, who famously loved playing video games and going to sleep, would agree with me, but instead she paused her braiding and gave me a look. Her gray eyes bore into mine.

She was waiting for me, I realized. She was waiting for me to ask her to braid my hair next, as I always did, as I hadn't yet. And I had an instinct, an unbidden knowing, that she'd started touching her own hair because she'd wanted me to ask her to touch mine. But then she turned sharply away. Her face colored, the rosacea on her cheeks pinkening. I hadn't asked fast enough. Worse, I'd caught her wanting me to ask.

"Aren't there things you want to have happen?" she said.

By which I imagined she meant, didn't I want to proceed into the next version of myself, whoever she was, to find out who I'd be once I'd dipped myself further into the frigid and thrilling waters of being alive? At fifteen, that meant pursuing any course of action unavailable to a child—doing anything that we wouldn't and couldn't have done before. Didn't I want to find out of what I was capable?

I did, but did it have to be right now? Only a week or two had passed since the end of school, and summer seemed to unfurl before me like an infinite golden carpet. We still had plenty of time to surprise ourselves.

Margaret finished her phone call, but she didn't immediately descend the stairs. Instead, we heard her walking around in the attic, her footsteps setting the wood floor to creak and groan through the house. A pause, then the sound of water rushing through the pipes. Then she came back down to the living room with a look on her face I didn't like.

"I know what we're doing tonight," she announced. "We're going out."

"We're going out?"

Her mom wasn't coming home. Nancy had spent the evening on a date and called to inform Margaret she wouldn't return until morning. Nancy didn't know her daughter had two friends preparing to sleep at her house, because she didn't know we were over at all. I didn't know Margaret's mom had begun going on dates. Did Eleanor? Margaret's parents' divorce wasn't even all the way finalized. My face burned.

"Let's walk to the Metropark," Margaret said.

"And what?" I asked.

"And like walk around."

The Metropark closed at eleven. It would be pitch-black. Once we got there, she'd make me stumble around in a marsh in the dark. I shook my head—please no. And yet, I saw real uneasiness and even fear on Margaret's face, reminding me suddenly of the time she'd read her mother's journal to me. The entry had been dated a year or two into Margaret's life. *I like myself less now than I did before,* it said. We laughed after Margaret read this

"Adults are dumb," she said.

I agreed. "Adults are literally so dumb." But I could tell she wished we hadn't read it

A fierce protectiveness rose up in me, a need to shield her from that desperate, sunken feeling, that unarticulated weight. I realized we couldn't just sit there. We'd have to follow her out of the house.

Margaret turned to Eleanor, and Eleanor said, "We could sleep at the high school. Like camping."

Then Eleanor gave Margaret a look that meant she obviously would have said yes to this adventure if it were just the two of them, and she gave me a look that meant, *I know you saw the look*

I just gave Margaret but you're not going to do better than this and you're welcome. The look meant, *Be grateful,* and I was.

We stuffed old pillows and picnic quilts into a couple of enormous synthetic blue bags, closed every window, locked and relocked every door, checked the garage, checked the attic just in case, set the house alarm, and made a run for it out the front door before the alarm could activate.

The sidewalks of Doan had darkened, gone hushed and tentative. We crept and slunk and whispered. After twenty minutes, we reached the low brick buildings of our high school, its parking lot empty. Margaret and Eleanor ran to the nearest structure and looked through its somber windows into its vacant classrooms. I hung back.

It's true that there wasn't anything more wrong with looking into an empty building than with standing outside it, but the whole night had taken on a presence I dared not disturb. I was sure I was about to be seen by someone, sure an eye would open on me. I lacked my friends' confidence in the ordinariness of the world, and I had to stop myself from calling them away. Margaret turned after a moment, ready for the next revelation, but El lingered, her eyes like sharpened pencils taking down a secret shape.

We kept walking, out beyond the school, past the track, to the far end of the soccer field, where a large hill rose with soft geometry from the ground. We made a bed for ourselves in the tall, wild grass, flung out our blankets and pillows into a single mattress. My silence had spread between us. We worked without speaking, the night like a place of worship. In the pure dark, we couldn't see the mosquitoes, so we pretended they weren't there.

Then, lying down on the blanket, the dark felt too large, so

Margaret started to wriggle around like a worm on the ground to make us laugh, and we pressed our heads together and whispered secrets about ourselves we all already knew. I sometimes read porn in the bathroom during dinner. Eleanor's famous first serve once hit a girl in the throat, and afterward the girl quit playing tennis. Margaret, alone in the kitchen last year, spilled water all over her mom's phone. When submerging it in rice failed to bring the phone back to life, she returned it to her mother's purse and said nothing. Margaret kept accidentally raising the volume of her voice as she thought of one more thing to say, and Eleanor kept reaching an arm across my torso to grab Margaret's wrist in reminder.

"Shh," she said over and over again. "Haven't you ever whispered in your life?"

Every time she hushed Margaret, Eleanor's breath heated my neck and the weight of her arm lay upon my stomach, and I felt perfect there between them. I noticed when El fell asleep, because her breath on my skin became even, and I lay there in the warm air of her exhalations wondering how long I could keep myself awake in this moment, how I could have more of it and what I thought the more might be.

"Mar," I whispered into the eerie dark. She adjusted her position next to me, so I knew she'd heard. "You put a penis in your mouth."

Her body shook against mine in silent laughter.

"Mina," she whispered back. "You broke a rule."

And she was right. I'd left the place I'd said I'd be without telling my mother, and I wasn't going to get up and go back, not now that I'd made it all the way here with my friends. All that remained for me was to sleep and then to wake up as a person who had already done this. Maple tree samaras spiraled down through the sky like falling eyelashes. I closed my eyes and wished on them.

I WOKE UP VERY EARLY in the morning, my forehead pressed to the curl of Margaret's back. Moisture clung to my face and hair, and droplets of dew bowed the blades of tall grass above me. Eleanor's body wasn't touching mine. I felt her missing from me and sat up.

She stood nearby, watching the sun rise, its ray like a brush combing the grassy field, her blanket in her hand. Her pale hair looked almost pink in the new light. Among it hung three small braids I hadn't seen her make the night before. The braids were loosened, fuzzed, plaits half released. I got up, immediately alert, my pulse tapping like rain. The braids were an invitation. I couldn't let her go home and unbraid them. I approached Eleanor. I was much taller than she was. Her mouth reached my shoulder. Her face, when it turned toward me, was soft with lingering sleep.

"Why do you always leave sleepovers early?" I asked, my voice low.

She looked at me with impatience. She looked at me a little bit like I was an idiot. She looked at me like she'd already come to a conclusion and all I had to do was allow it.

And then she was kissing me—one hand to my waist, the other rising to touch my neck, to lower my face to hers—her lips on mine—her lips on mine—spectacular and disappearing as a snowflake.

Margaret rolled over and made a noise as though she might

wake up. I thought Margaret could go ahead and die! But already Eleanor was withdrawing.

Her face flashed with superlative vulnerability. I had never seen such a look on her face before, and I knew right away she'd hold my having seen it against me. I stiffened. The idea of Eleanor holding anything against me had become suddenly intolerable.

For a minute we just stood there watching Margaret's face, watching her eyes move behind her eyelids but never open and feeling like if they did it might be the end of the world. If she'd seen us, then what? And if she hadn't, to resume our usual three-way dynamic in the aftermath of what had happened felt impossible, almost violent.

"Tell Mar I said bye when she wakes up," Eleanor said.

I nodded. I wanted her to stay, and I wanted her to leave, so that I could be alone for a moment and try to understand what had transpired between us. I watched her outline recede through the field and finally disappear. For long minutes, I remained where I was, busy being rearranged by the effect of her mouth on mine.

Then I woke Margaret and reported Eleanor's having already left, and we gathered our remaining pillows and blankets into our bags and walked back to her house through the grass, dew dripping down my legs and mosquito bites swelling my ankles.

I ENTERED MY HOUSE ON A CLOUD. I HAD BEEN KISSED. OTHER truths belonged on the ground where they had nothing to do with me. I could have run up to my room but didn't. I could have said nothing but I was bad at being quiet. I texted Eleanor an emoji of a sunrise. I traipsed into the kitchen. My mother wasn't there. I continued into the living room and found her folding laundry. I fell upon the tuffet of waiting towels, still warm from the dryer.

She wanted my help, naturally. I picked up a towel and folded it in half and then in half again.

"No. Let me show you," she said, and began demonstrating for the hundredth time her method of thirds.

"Stop," I said, and sat down on the arm of the couch. "I want to tell you something." I didn't mean to be dramatic. I just couldn't immediately say the words. "Eleanor kissed me in the field behind the school last night—this morning."

My mom looked at me from above her towel.

"She kissed you."

"Yes." She kissed me. I wanted to print the words on a billboard. I wanted to wear them on a T-shirt.

"In the field behind the school, this morning."

"Yes."

"Why were you in the field behind the school? It's only seven. What time was this?"

Here was the point at which I could have lied but didn't.

"Because we slept there," I said, almost angrily, because I already knew by then where we were going.

"You were supposed to sleep at Margaret's."

I stood up. "I was very near Margaret's. I was fine. I wasn't at a party. No one else was there, only the three of us. I'm trying to tell you about like a life event." My body was getting very hot.

"You told me you would be at Margaret's, and then instead you were somewhere else. You weren't even at a house. You were in the middle of a field"—she didn't need to say, a field where anyone could have scooped me up and driven me blindfolded across state lines or into a shallow grave or the mouths of coyotes—"which is something I would not have agreed to, had you asked me, which you did not."

Having said all this, she looked as though she were about to resume folding the towel, so I pulled it out of her hands and threw it on the ground. "Could you stop doing laundry for like one minute of your life?"

She didn't like that at all. She removed a strand of hair that had stuck to her face.

"I didn't ask permission, but I didn't have to tell you either. Everything was fine. Everything was completely fine. I slept on some grass and walked home. I'm telling you right now, of my own volition, because I wanted you to know. I could have said nothing!"

I burst into tears. Nothing had ever happened to me, and now one single thing had happened to me, and I'd shown it to her, and she was ruining it. She was corroding its perfect surface every second we stood there together having a fight instead of a high five.

"I'm the good one," I said, my voice plaintive and desperate. I refused to wipe the hot water from my face. "You don't know how good I am. I'm the responsible one. I say no to everything. I'm the least fun person I know, and it's all for you!"

She had no idea what this meant, and I couldn't explain it to her. I couldn't tell her all the times I'd stopped my friends from being reckless without revealing their recklessness. I couldn't put myself into context without making her want to take me away from my life. And it wouldn't have mattered anyway—she never judged my character against the rubric of anyone else's behavior, only her own standard of right.

"You've broken my trust," she said in a straightforward tone of voice that asked me to hear what she meant, but I had no desire to understand.

"You've broken my trust," I shouted back. "I'll just lie to you from now on. I'll just tell you nothing. My friends don't tell their moms anything. No one does! It's just me, and I won't anymore." I considered this a very grave threat. Just saying it out loud made me ache. But her face hardly moved. I hated that nothing appeared to be wrong with her, that her expression could remain so neutral. I couldn't understand it, I who wore my feelings like clothes and could hide nothing.

"Aren't you going to say one friendly thing?"

She straightened her shoulders, collecting herself. "It's wonderful that you and Eleanor kissed," she said. "It is. I'm glad for you. I should have said that first. Congratulations."

The words coming out of her mouth were so measured, so discordant with my pinnacle of feeling. I began to spin away from her in disgust.

"Mina," she said, and I stopped. She almost looked apologetic. If she felt sorry, it was for what she had to say next, which was that she was going to call Margaret's and Eleanor's parents and tell them what we'd done.

I RAN AWAY TO MY room, and it didn't feel far enough. I sat in my closet to have more doors between us, and the gesture felt stupid. I felt stupid. My emotions crested above my head and fell on top of me like a bucket of cold water. I texted Margaret and Eleanor what was happening because I had to.

IM SORRY, I wrote.

I didn't report the exact contents of my conversation with my mother, just what they could expect from her and why. I did make it clear that I'd told her about the field on my own, that I'd manufactured our mutual demise for no reason. She'd forced no explanation from me. We hadn't been caught; I'd given us away. Guilt and shame beat their fists against the windows of my heart, and I knew they wouldn't stop until I told my friends the whole of what I'd done. I was desperate to get it over with, so I could feel better. I sent a bunch of messages in a row. The chat looked wildly lopsided, all my blue text filling up the right side of the screen.

Maybe I should have called them on the phone or on video, so they could have seen my dumb miserable face, but I couldn't bear to be looked at by Eleanor so immediately under such dramatically worse circumstances, and I didn't want to be seen by Margaret either.

ahhhh ok, Margaret responded. A minute later she sent, *lemme go deal.*

And then she said nothing else. Eleanor sent nothing at all. I assumed they were talking to their moms and also to each other, in a separate text, which they had a right to do, which I would have done if I were them, but I wanted to dig a hole in the ground and live there for the rest of my life. I needed someone to tell about my misery, but usually I told my friends about my mom and my mom about my friends, so I wrote a very long note for myself in my phone in order to avoid further exacerbating the word-count ratio in our group chat. The note was full of self-loathing because given the same circumstances, I knew I'd make the same mistake again. Then I put my phone into a shoe.

I was the least chill person on earth and I knew it. Everyone else had a skeleton, and I was just a bunch of organs. I couldn't keep a single thing to myself if it mattered. I needed to leash myself like a dog. I needed to tell myself to sit or I'd show everybody my belly.

I tried instead to remember the kiss in its perfection, my body as it had been, but every minute that passed took me further and further away from the self I'd been in the moment El had kissed me. The self I was now, in my closet, would not have been kissed. Had it really happened? Was there any reason in the world to believe it had happened beyond my own memory of it? I took my phone back out of the shoe and realized I hadn't taken any pictures by the school or in the field. My last images were of the three of us, on Margaret's street, the golden light still cradling our faces.

The clock on my phone read 8:00. Somehow, the whole rest of the day remained for me to further ruin my own life. I needed time to pass faster, so I crawled into bed and went to sleep for a few hours. When I woke, my mom came in to inform me that the calls had been made; Nancy and Kim said they were grateful to my mom for reporting their daughters' misconduct.

They weren't really, or they weren't especially. They could have done without the information, I later heard from Margaret, though neither of them would have admitted as much to my grave and upright mother.

Nancy was mostly embarrassed, and she yelled at Margaret for embarrassing her. Margaret shouted back that it was embarrassing her mother had sex sleepovers with random men while she was in the middle of having wholesome, childhood sleepovers with her friends. They screamed at each other for a while about whose behavior was least becoming and who had the right to criticize whom.

It could have been worse, however. My mom thought we'd snuck out while Nancy slept in her bed. She thought Nancy had been duped by us, instead of absent, because I hadn't told her Nancy wasn't there. Not out of virtue—I'd simply failed to say so, and then we were in the middle of our fight. Nancy didn't correct her either. She would have been humiliated by my mom knowing, or by having to inform her, that we'd been left alone unsupervised on account of her dating life. But considering that mention of her absence had never been made, considering that nothing actually bad had happened—no abuse of substances, no fraternizing with the opposite sex, no breaking of family heirlooms, et cetera—considering that Nancy was a very busy person with a real and demanding job and an almost ex-ed husband and a romantic life she was attempting to restart for the sake of her dignity, she decided her daughter had to spend the rest of the weekend cleaning out their scary basement, and that was about it.

Eleanor's mom had an even more circumspect attitude.

"Maybe you should let me know the next time you plan to go camping," was all Kim said. Then she went back to designing somebody's chic living room. Her daughter could randomly decide to sleep in a field if she felt like it. Eleanor had her phone set to share her GPS location and a sound head on her shoulders. She was a teenager, after all, and could have done worse. Her siblings had all done worse. That's what Eleanor told Margaret had happened, and then Margaret told me. Eleanor didn't tell me herself because she didn't respond to my texts at all.

I REMAINED AWAKE LATE THAT night, aware I wouldn't be able to go anywhere in the morning. I sat on top of my comforter and stared out the window beside my bed. Huge trees obscured the world beyond my backyard. Only partially visible above them hung the moon. Was she sorry for me? It seemed possible. The blackened palette of night blunted reality.

Still, I felt deeply shaken by what I'd missed in myself. Prior to Eleanor kissing me, I would not have said that the nature of my friendship with her differed from the nature of my friendship with Margaret—only that Eleanor and Margaret were themselves different people, and that our friendships therefore manifested differently. An inadequate characterization, apparently. Eleanor had proven that by kissing me—I, though I hadn't known it yet, by wanting so badly to be kissed.

I should have known. I should have noticed. I hadn't considered Eleanor a person I could kiss. Because she was a girl, yes, but even more so because she was a person I already loved and had loved for years. The sexual interactions of my life thus far had exclusively involved people who weren't important to me. They could be easily discarded. In middle school, I'd had a boyfriend I never talked to. We served a purpose for each other. Kissing Eleanor could not serve a tidy purpose for me. Kissing Eleanor radically reoriented my inner life.

The rest of that weekend, I wasn't able to help myself. I texted her. When she didn't respond, I sent more messages. I sent too many. I said I wanted to kiss again. I apologized for getting her into trouble, even though I hadn't, in case she'd feel compelled to reassure me. I sent references to the sun, to the field, the occasional lone emoji as though I might catch her off guard. I sent a screenshot of Sim Ginevra's baby, whom I had aged up to be a purple-haired toddler of perfect computer cuteness. I cropped the image to exclude the baby's name, so that she might ask me what it was, but she didn't. I texted in our usual style in case she was waiting for a sign of my willingness to ignore what had happened, but she wasn't. Not that I would have been able to hold my tongue had she sent me even one neutral text, which she did not.

On Sunday night, I deleted all those messages from my phone, just to hide from the shame of having sent them, to avoid looking at the long, lopsided screenplay of my unanswered texts. But then the trouble was, it was like I'd never sent them in the first place, because there was no proof I had—beyond my humiliation, which lingered persistently, without the grounding effect of evidence and without relief.

El's silence forced me to conclude that whatever she'd wanted from me at the time, before I'd gone and ruined it, she didn't want anymore. I'd proven myself unready. And yet, when she posted a picture of herself in a bikini sitting by her pool only a few hours after she would have received my last message, I couldn't help feeling the photo was directed at me and taking it personally.

I COULDN'T SLEEP THAT NIGHT. I DIDN'T WANT TO HAVE TO WAKE UP in daylight and be expected to eat breakfast or answer questions. Had my life changed, or not? I turned off all the lights in my bedroom and got into bed naked. I lifted my laptop onto my chest and determined to spend the next six hours submerged in the Technicolor balm of animated television. I put on my favorite show. Unfortunately, it was also Eleanor's and reminded me inevitably of the start of our friendship.

I met Eleanor when our lower schools pooled into a single campus for seventh and eighth grade. She had her own preexisting friends, but none of them close. She was aloof but too pretty to be ostracized. She had a complete set of rainbow gel pens, but she didn't like to share them. Other kids found this off-putting. She attended birthday parties and playdates without becoming anybody's best anything.

Margaret claimed Eleanor as our friend first. I didn't want to share Margaret any more than she already insisted on being shared, but my being against it did very little to slow the start of our friendship. Margaret and Eleanor bonded through a shared willingness for truancy. They both lied for a week straight about having their periods in order to avoid swimming for gym. Our school had a frigid, acerbically chlorinated pool. Every class was obligated, at some point, to take swimming as a gym rotation. The school considered buoyancy a life skill, or they wanted to justify the district's financial investment in an enormous rectangle of cold water.

On any given pool day, at least one kid claimed to have an ear infection or an upset stomach. The pervasiveness of the impulse to skip meant that all excuses were met with skepticism from the gym teacher—except for having your period. Having your period didn't require a doctor's note and repelled questions from adults with and without uteruses. No one wanted to tell a twelve-year-old to put in a tampon. The only downside of the excuse was its time limit, a week tops. After that, everyone would think you had some sort of monster biological functions, because everyone did know the meaning of a girl's otherwise unexplained abstention from swimming. This was embarrassing enough to prevent the full eighth of the class who might have actually been menstruating from saying so. Willingness to use a period as either a ruse or a real excuse implied a level of confidence with your own reproductive happenings that was rare among us. I remember resenting Margaret and Eleanor for that confidence as much as I initially resented their togetherness.

The rest of us, maybe forty at a time, swam laps or splashed behind kickboards or floated on our backs, covertly butterflying our hands to stay afloat. So many small flapping bodies set the water into a chaos of intersecting waves. I was a good swimmer, which made me too proud to swim in the shallow end, where I would certainly have been less miserable. Instead, I swam in the deep end, where I felt overwhelmed by arms and legs on either side of me and was unable to easily touch my toes to the bottom of the pool and rest, in spite of my already advancing height.

To be made, in the middle of the day, to strip down to a one-piece bathing suit in front of everyone you know and then emerge forty-five minutes later, sopping wet and shivering with red goggle rims around your eyes, is undignified, but no one cares about the dignity of a twelve-year-old. Of course, I couldn't tolerate exempting myself from an obligation. I couldn't lie to the gym teacher about blood falling out of my vagina. So I had to swim, and Margaret and Eleanor didn't.

They spent their vacation from the water sitting together high up on the yellow wood bleachers. I saw their heads turning continually to speak to each other, their mouths to each other's ears, probably so they could hear over the din of the water and the complaints of the swimmers and the chastisements of the gym teacher reminding us not to stop between laps. After class, I'd ask Margaret what they talked about, but she had nothing to report other than that she liked Eleanor and thought I would too.

Five days is not very long in adult time, but a school week is sufficient to change the life of a barely teenaged person. By Friday, Margaret had solidified her claim on Eleanor by inviting her to our weekend sleepover. Naturally, I was alarmed. Constant vigilance, really, is necessary to hold on to your friends at that age. Not that I thought Margaret would throw me off. We were too deeply bound. Half of her pairs of underwear were mine that she'd never given back. But I might become her old, default best friend, her obligatory childhood best friend, instead of her shiny, chosen, new best friend—which I intended to avoid.

At the sleepover, Margaret left us alone in her room for a while to go placate her mother about some recent inflammatory behavior on the part of her father. Eleanor and I sat on the floor in our pajamas. The conversation turned to TV.

"Serena can't be your favorite," I said. "She's Sailor Moon." I considered choosing the show's protagonist an abdication of the responsibility of expressing a favorite. Eleanor called Sailor Moon by her Japanese name, Usagi, before realizing I wasn't familiar.

"Alright," she said, and considered. "Then, Sailor Uranus."

Known to me as Amara, Sailor Uranus split her time between contributing to the group effort to protect the planet from sexy and thematic alien invasions and pursuing a career as a professional teenaged race car driver. She was tall and wore button-down shirts and spent all her time with her cousin, Sailor Neptune, known to me as Michelle. But Sailor Uranus and Sailor Neptune were secondary members of the cast. They only appeared in a subset of the show's total episodes. As a result, I thought Eleanor had become annoyed with me for refuting her original answer and so chosen the character with the funniest name.

"Mine is Mars," I said.

Sailor Mars had amazing long black hair and was mad at everyone all the time.

"Ugh," Eleanor sighed in agreement. "Yes, totally."

What I wanted from Eleanor was proof that she understood the primacy of my friendship with Margaret. That she wanted to be our friend—my friend too—but also would be fine with Margaret and me hanging out without her, as we had done for a decade. At that age, it's dangerous to befriend anyone who too obviously wants to hang out with you. Adults instructed us, especially the girls, to *be nice* as a blanket statement without understanding the tight social confines in which we lived. No one could get away from anyone else, having nowhere to go and no way of pretending you were busy. There weren't any boundaries except for the ones that we ourselves enforced when it came to the couple of hundred people we saw all day, five days a week, for three quarters of the year. There was so little space in the social life of that era that every new friendliness was essentially a threat to the existing version of peace. I didn't want to create any obligations of friendship that I would then feel compelled to follow through on unless I was sure I wanted the friend.

I offered to draw Uranus's symbol on the flesh of Eleanor's inner arm with a permanent marker if she would draw Mars's symbol on mine. By the time Margaret came back, we were covered in squiggles. She pouted, so we drew all over her next. When Margaret inscribed an inside joke of ours on my leg with the black pen, Eleanor didn't ask what it meant or suggest she wanted the same. She let Margaret's claim on me stand because she was smart and because she was proud. She was aware that we were desirable friends to have at school, but there were other desirable groups she could have attempted to join instead—and didn't. We accepted Eleanor as ours because it was clear to us that she would be. In the wake of the kiss, it occurred to me that in addition to being ours, she might also be mine.

At the time of my first sleepover with Eleanor, I had watched and rewatched the old nineties English dub of *Sailor Moon* through an illegal video-streaming service that required you to take a break every seventy-two minutes or give them your credit card. To my outrage, the prompt to pay usually fell at some point in the middle of an episode. Three years later, I figured there had to be a better option. A bit of searching led me to discover subtitled versions of the episodes that were also available to stream for free online. The subtitles hewed much more closely to the original Japanese audio, which the network had heavily censored in its dubbing for American audiences based on what they deemed appropriate for children. In my bed in the middle of the night, I found out that Amara's and Michelle's real names were Haruka and Michiru. Also, Haruka and Michiru weren't cousins. They were in love.

Blood moved hard through my body. I reviewed what I knew: They blushed at each other, they held hands, and Haruka liked to drive Michiru around in her yellow convertible sports car. Now that I was paying attention, the two of them were very obviously boning. Eleanor, I realized for not the first time, was much better than I was at using the computer.

THREE WEEKS IS AN ETERNITY IN THE SUMMER, AND THAT'S HOW long my mom forbade me from having sleepovers or seeing my friends, though she never actually named this duration for my punishment. When I asked how long I had to stay at home, she said she didn't know. She said she'd tell me when she figured it out—which was like her, not to punish me with any numerical certitude but instead with her infinite, ongoing measurement of my worth.

She thought I should use this time productively. She thought I should sign up for an activity. But I refused. Instead, I stomped around the house and closed all my drawers with dramatic flourish and force. If I signed up for an activity, she'd be able to plausibly conclude that punishing me led to an expansion of my horizons, which I could not allow. I didn't want her to feel justified in exerting more control over me when I so badly wanted her to exert less. Of course, at the same time, I was hoping she wouldn't change at all. So I had to remain at home all day every day with her for as long as the interval of her anger turned out to be—weeks, months, the whole summer, who knew.

Eleanor didn't text me back, and eventually I stopped texting her. Day after day passed in digital silence. She had incredible control over herself for a person of that age, likely on account of having grown up in the wake of so many adult siblings. She'd had to count on herself to provide her own entertainment. This was one of the things I'd loved about her from the start, her magnetized pillar of self—that you could throw yourself against her and would rebound. For the same reason she couldn't play team sports, I wanted to be her friend. I'd accepted her into what existed between myself and Margaret, after almost ten years of best friendship without a third, and now I had to accept the consequences. I had to accept I'd thrown myself against her, and I'd rebounded.

"Now is a good opportunity to go through your closet," my mom suggested over breakfast. It was eight o'clock in the morning, five days after Eleanor kissed me. I gave her a look of vile loathing.

"You need to learn how to be alone," she said to me.

"Because you're so self-reliant," I countered, and then felt like a monster. She didn't have a job other than me. "Fine, we can do it," I said. Because I'd just insulted her for no reason, I felt I had to agree.

My mom blew on her hot spoonful of un-sugared oatmeal and then put it in her mouth and chewed. Did she consider me a rude and heavy backpack she was obligated to carry up a hill? This was a new thought, and though I asked myself the question, I lacked the capacity to appreciate its possible answers.

After we finished our meal, I followed her upstairs to my bedroom, where I put on and took off all my clothing piece by piece while she sat on my bed and we both looked at me in the large mirror mounted on my wall. I liked how I looked, but I thought I could like myself even more with certain alterations, if only I could figure out what they were. Something to do with my hair and manner of expression and thighs and sense of style and way of standing and nose and which pairs of pants I owned and also my face.

I moved my phone from my dresser to my bedside table, screen-side down next to my cloud lamp. Because my mom didn't take away my phone or my computer as part of my punishment, I periodically had to take them away from myself. I couldn't tolerate the minute-to-minute continuous confirmation that Eleanor still hadn't said anything. Especially given that if she did decide to text me, for the sake of my dignity, I'd have to wait at least an hour before responding. I liked to imagine I was getting a head start.

I tried on a tank top with finger-width straps and a high, square neckline that my mom had made me buy against my will the year before. Annoyingly, the top now looked good on me. I turned my torso to the left and right in the mirror, wanting to see myself over my shoulder. I put my fingers in my hair and shook it out. Late June was humid, and I welcomed the movement of air on my neck. My mom had pinned her hair into a twist. Her arms were bare, her watch on her wrist, her nails unpainted. She looked like she approved of my appearance, so I felt a great yearning to disagree. I smothered the instinct, still in a state of recoil from my recent cruelty. Then I changed into a triangular dress I wanted to get rid of.

My mom picked up its hem, shrinking the length by a good four inches.

"We could have it altered," she said. "Or wait until you grow."

I hated that my mom seemed to know where I was heading ahead of time. It wasn't fair she could pick clothes for a body that didn't exist yet when I had so little sense myself of who I might become. I wanted to know what I would eventually look like and where on the spectrum of attractiveness I could reasonably expect myself to arrive.

It bothered me that I couldn't be an impartial judge of

myself. I could merely watch for whatever changes took hold in me. I could merely part my hair down the middle and then the side and then the middle again in an attempt to discern which looked best. I had wanted armpit hair up until the moment it arrived, and then I wanted it to go away again. My breasts, alas, were arriving unevenly. Sometimes I'd talk to the smaller one, urging it, in a kindly voice, to hurry the fuck up.

I walked over to my bedside table and turned my phone right side up. The lock screen illuminated empty. I turned it over again.

"You'll never be the most beautiful person you know," my mom had once told me. "No one is. Everyone always knows someone else."

Upon hearing this, I felt both terribly sad and also deeply reassured.

Over and over, we negotiated my body. What looked good on me and what didn't. The right to wear my hair unbrushed or wet. The right to forget sunscreen and accidentally burn myself to a crisp in Eleanor's backyard. The features I'd inherited from her—what she did with them versus what I did with them. The genetically stubborn black circles beneath our eyes that she covered up with concealer every morning. I thought they made me look moody, like I was in the aftermath of a party—an effect worth cultivating seeing that it was basically never true.

She didn't make strict rules. I didn't have to wear knee-length skirts or get her permission on my social media posts. But she had opinions about every inch of my person, and I knew what all of them were and could not unknow them. For this reason, I never wanted to speak Eleanor's name to her again. Whatever she said, I'd never be able to un-hear.

I handed the triangle dress to my mother, who notably did not place the item in the donation pile. Next, I tried on a pair of shorts that were obviously too small for me but that I refused to get rid of because they looked good too small. I liked when my legs looked like cartoon legs. My mom was skeptical but wary of inflaming me further during such a delicate operation.

"Those are good weekend shorts," she said.

"There's no real dress code at school," I replied. "I could wear these if I wanted to." I probably wouldn't, though. I'd stand in front of the dresser holding the shorts and wonder if she was right and lose confidence.

Rain began to fall outside, pattering on the roof. My phone vibrated. My mom sat back down on my bed, anticipating that I'd want to check my messages, but now that I knew for sure a notification awaited me, I wanted to open it alone.

"I'm keeping them," I said of the shorts, and then dismissed myself and my phone to the bathroom. The notification was a weather alert: It had in fact begun to rain. Useless. Peeing, I scrolled through my feed. First the algorithm fed me a meme from *The Sims* of a woman sitting at a desk in a bath towel playing a video game while her baby lies on the ground beside her on fire. Next appeared a picture Margaret had posted of Eleanor standing in a parking lot in front of a black SUV. She wore an extra-large crewneck sweatshirt, a miniskirt, and her hair pulled up into a high ponytail tied tight enough to change the angles of her face. I checked both Eleanor's and Margaret's profiles for additional content, but neither had posted anything else. I'd once been afraid of losing Margaret to Eleanor, and now I was forced to consider the pain of losing Eleanor to Margaret.

I looked at the picture one more time, then opened my web browser and navigated to the tab I never closed and read one of my favorite chapters of Ginevra, in which the fairy journeys deep within a mystic cave to bathe in its healing waters. While she bathes, the waters part to reveal a pearl wand. The pearl wand thrums with ancient power. This power will enable Ginevra to resolve certain pressing political conflicts that plague her realm, but first she lies down on a rock adjacent to the pool and uses the wand to fuck herself until she comes thirteen times, and after the thirteenth time, she sleeps, and while she sleeps, a beautiful pearlescent mist spreads over the adjacent village, causing its inhabitants to ascend into a divine orgy that lasts for thirteen days and thirteen nights. And when Ginevra wakes and emerges from the cave, everyone is pregnant with babies obviously destined to be born with their own magical powers, and the village worships Ginevra as their new goddess, and she is like, *Sure, why not?* and then flies away on her lilac wings.

I can go back to my room, I told myself. *I can go try on some more clothes and be nice to my mother.*

THE NEXT WEEK STORMED. DAMP MORNINGS CONDENSED INTO tempestuous afternoons. Claps of thunder shook the house and between them hung silences vibrating with significance. When it wasn't raining, I went for runs around the neighborhood. I didn't pass directly in front of Eleanor's house, because I had some dignity to preserve, but I ran along the streets nearby such that she might see me anyway with my chest going up and down and my braided ponytail swishing between my shoulder blades. That was how I would have liked to be seen by her, so I also felt certain that I wouldn't be, which was its own source of comfort. To run along drunk on the idea of my own attractiveness and untested by its reality.

When I got home, I didn't allow myself to look into any reflective surfaces until after I'd taken a shower. I didn't want to find out that my face was bright red and my hair a fuzzy ring. Sometimes it's better to be nice to yourself by not knowing things. And during those days, I was especially in need of my own kindness.

Once complete silence had been established on our personal thread, Eleanor began to respond, briefly, sporadically, to the messages I sent our group chat, but only after Margaret had also already said something, so that even in digital space we were never so much as briefly alone together, which of course was worse than not texting me at all, because it prevented me from imagining that she'd put her phone in a blender or thrown it off a cliff. I hated seeing her name show up on my phone screen and having to wonder for even one second if this time she'd sent the message to just me and then feeling disappointed when she hadn't. I tried to compensate by brushing my hair elaborately in front of the mirror for twenty minutes at a time.

On one of my runs, I ran into Margaret. She had a sleepover bag slung over her shoulder and a look on her face that I wouldn't have called happy. It dissolved into a false smile as soon as she saw me, the kind of smile she wore when she didn't want to explain herself to someone.

"Hi!" she exclaimed from across the street. I'd apologized repeatedly for getting her into trouble, mostly via text message but also once over the phone. I'd tried sincerely, irreverently, and in manners burdened by self-loathing to communicate how sorry I was to have put her in that position, but none of these apologies seemed to work the way they should have, because Margaret accepted and dismissed them without actually convincing me to feel better. Her texts were terse, in both the group chat and our own thread. She'd hurried me off the phone and never called back.

"How are you?" I asked moments later with my arms around her neck and my face in her hair, warm from the sun that had emerged in the aftermath of the most recent downpour. "I'm so sorry, seriously," I added, in case she needed to hear it from me in person. I sensed I'd have to stop apologizing soon. The *sorrys* themselves had become unwelcome. She waved this one off with a hand.

"How are you doing?" she asked me back without answering for herself.

"All my Sims are thriving," I said. "Really living their best lives."

I hated being in a fight with Margaret, because she never admitted to being in a fight with me. She fought with her mother by shouting, but she fought with everyone else by pretending it wasn't happening. She picked up her bag from the sidewalk and looked in the direction of her house.

"Do you want to come in?" she asked.

My face contorted, I'm sure. A sick hesitancy flushed through me. Entering her house would have been a deliberate break from the terms set by my mother. She wouldn't ever find out, but still I couldn't lie to her, not even by omission, as Margaret was well aware.

"Oh my God, I wish," I said, playing dumb. "Really soon though, I hope."

She looked me in the eye for half a second and then laughed. Laughter sometimes served as Margaret's version of a confrontation. She already knew what I would and wouldn't do; she'd merely been pointing it out.

"Moms aren't the law," she once said to me, and I sat there in silence because my mom was. Margaret's mom had a personal life. Mine didn't, not that I could see. Her mom's personal life produced visible decisions that Margaret could critique, choices that Margaret could use to justify her various rebellions. My mom's personal life seemed entirely beyond my purview. To me, my mom remained an icon. To Margaret, her mom was just a woman telling her what to do. Her mom was a woman sleeping with at least one man who wasn't her father, and Margaret had chosen not to tell me.

I walked home very fast with tears in my eyes. The sun was a hot rock in the sky. My armpits and neck prickled with sweat. I wanted to get off the sidewalk and indoors as soon as possible. Even though my mom hardly used air-conditioning—she liked when the air inside the house matched the air outside the house and only turned it on at night if my dad couldn't sleep—our interior still felt chilly compared to the blazing heat outdoors. All our ceiling fans were set to whir, the continuous swish of their blades a symptom of summer as I knew it. I stood in the kitchen and drank a glass of ice water and held the cold cup to my cheeks and prayed my mother wasn't about to walk into the room and read misery on my face and ask me about it.

I hated seeing her every day of my punishment, eating breakfast and lunch just the two of us at the table, then dinner together with my father once he got home from work. She didn't seem like other people to me. She was serious. She was morally upright. She didn't procrastinate. She didn't have outbursts. She drank only on holidays. She read the news without acquiring any knowledge of pop culture. She'd wanted more children and miscarried many. Her mother had died in a car crash when my mom was in her twenties. Why did she have to be who she was, not the same as other mothers, and who was she turning me into as a result—not the same as other girls?

During those weeks of confinement, I felt the edges of this childlike complaint crumbling away before the arrival of a greater and uninvited nuance in my understanding of my mother as a person. This nuance pressed upon me most in her presence, so I tried to avoid being together. Unfortunately, she entered the kitchen in spite of my wishing with a book in her hand and looked surprised to see me, as though either of us could actually lose the other in the house where we lived. She ignored the ornery tone of my voice when I said so.

"You're always in your room lately," she explained.

The two of us seemed more mixed up in each other than my friends did with their mothers. My mom never lied to me, rarely even by omission. She told me about the physical realities of sex early, as she imagined they might apply to me. She wouldn't let me win games as a child, and she wouldn't say she liked an outfit if she didn't.

"Today could be the day we work on the weeds," she said.

"Today could be the day I light myself on fire," I replied.

I refused to pretend to be fine, because I couldn't bear the thought of her believing me. She gave me a judicious look. I knew she didn't want to work on the weeds either.

"You always want me to do things at the worst possible moment of my life," I said.

"In what way is this the worst possible moment of your life?"

"I'm not telling you."

I wanted to tell her. And also, she couldn't be allowed to know. I wanted her to yell at me and for both of our heads to bang together until I felt better, but she didn't.

"How's—" she began, and I knew the next word out of her mouth would be either *Eleanor* or *Margaret*, so I fled to the living room and flung myself onto the couch. She didn't follow or defend herself, no fisticuffs. Rather than fight with her daughter, she weathered me. My electric storms of feeling routinely coalesced and dispersed. She had only to wait, and she was a woman of interminable patience.

I looked around the living room. Family photographs crowded the walls: aunts and uncles naked and smiling in the park as babies, my father sporting a beard I'd never seen in real life, my parents at their wedding, the glass crushed beneath their feet. And my mother by herself too: a sly child wearing saddle shoes and full dresses; lying upside down on a couch with her head dangling off the edge; maybe sixteen in a white two-piece bathing suit, laughing as a wave of cold ocean water hit her bare legs.

I had a funny relationship with these pictures. They seemed to me like exposition in a movie about my mother, like they existed to provide her with backstory rather than as evidence of a person named Celeste who had actually lived through every moment represented on that wall and the infinite unrecorded moments that surrounded them too. That Celeste was once childless, unmarried, overwhelmed, filled with lust or anger or loneliness, once wishing she could drive, once happy and bare in a swimsuit, once known to her friends only as C—these were facts that seemed to slide off the surface of me whenever I came into contact with them. I turned my face in to the couch pillow and closed my eyes.

THE FOURTH OF JULY FELL ON A TUESDAY THAT YEAR. THE HOLIDAY presented a problem for me in its undeniability as an occasion for seeing people. Everyone would be going out and posting about it. Everyone would be wearing outfits. Eleanor would be going out and wearing an outfit. And still, I hadn't heard from her.

What Margaret would have advised me to do, had I been in a position to receive her advice, was to post a very fire photo of myself. So I elaborately composed my hair and makeup in the bathroom for as many hours as I could stretch the activity, while listening to music and slinking around in front of the mirror, making eyes and cheeks at myself, examining myself from various degrees of profile, raising and lowering my chin and eyelashes, opening and closing my mouth, occasionally singing. In these kinds of wars, you have to make clear to the other party that your hotness cannot be ignored, that your hotness is inherent to the situation at hand and ongoing, and if you want to occupy the hottest version of yourself, then you have to call her up and out.

I faced the mirror with my hair blown dry and my eyeliner applied and stood on my tiptoes, and it felt possible that I could will Eleanor into texting me back by means of my face and body, even before I took the picture. That my hotness could curl the ribbon between us, and Eleanor would feel it from the other side.

Then I kissed the cold mirror with my eyes open, in case I could see what I'd done wrong when I kissed Eleanor with my eyes closed. Then I licked it.

I took my picture in the driveway instead of the garden because the driveway suggested a second location. Yes, it could have been considered pathetic to post a picture of myself that implied I was going somewhere when I wasn't, but all of us basically did that all of the time. And more importantly, whatever I posted would definitely appear at the top of Eleanor's feed, as all of her and Margaret's posts always appeared at the top of mine, and I wanted to be hot in front of Eleanor more than I cared about anything else. If Eleanor was going to pretend not to have kissed me, then I wanted to remind her that this was the person she was pretending not to have kissed.

I situated myself beneath the power lines that loped above the sidewalk of my street. Right away, sweat rose to my surface. Clouds made an oven of the late-afternoon air, but an intermittent light also touched the neighborhood, sparkling off the hoods of cars and sharpening the shadows of leaves thrown onto the streets by the trees above them. Inside my house, I felt safe, but I also felt stranded. Out here I could hear all the insects, the swelling ambient noise of the season. A woodpecker thrummed against one of the trees on my street, and a jackhammer somewhere in the surrounding blocks operated in fifteen-second bursts. If I strained, I could hear the faint tinkling music of an ice-cream truck.

This was why I came outside so often. The perfect splendor of Ohio high summer articulated my aloneness back to me in gold script. It said that I was experiencing a trial of the heart. I was being shunned by my first lover. I had the right to a grandeur of melancholy previously unknown to me, and this right made me feel beautiful.

I set up my tripod on the cement and used a timer to take my picture. I posed with one of my hands in my hair, then on my hip, resetting my phone over and over again. I arched my back, tilted my head, and changed the angle of my shoulders. Eventually, I felt an awareness and turned to see a rabbit standing on its hind legs on the tree lawn fifteen feet in front of me, belly exposed. Its black eye met mine, all pupil, before it dashed across the street.

"Are you going somewhere?" my mom asked me when I returned to the house through the side door a few minutes later wearing nine layers of mascara and a crop top.

"No," I said, and I made a bowl of cereal and carried it back upstairs to my room to eat while I looked through the two hundred photos of myself I'd taken and decided which one to post.

happy 4th! I texted Margaret.

happy 4th!! she sent back an hour later.

I watched the fireworks from the end of the block with my parents and our neighbors. I didn't want to walk to the field behind the school where the real show took place because my friends would be there, and even though my mom would surely have let me say hello or even watch the fireworks with them, I'd still have to go home at the end of the night, and the two of them would leave together. Also I couldn't bear to stand again on that same field where Eleanor had kissed me, now that we were estranged and what had happened between us had gone unacknowledged.

I waited until the next morning to post my content and then waited another three hours for Margaret to post hers. First a picture of herself and Bea in various states of patriotic undress, standing in front of the black SUV I now recognized as Bea's car.

And then a second picture of herself with Eleanor, who had her arm around Bea's best friend, Olivia.

Eleanor was wearing my shirt, pale-blue pointelle. The one I'd lent Margaret. The shirt cast a triangular shadow, lifting as it did from the skin above Eleanor's belly button.

THE NEXT DAY MY MOM INSISTED WE GO TO THE GROCERY STORE. She went to the grocery store what felt like fifty times a week, and she considered me, for the duration of my punishment, available at any moment to accompany her. Which I interpreted as one more form of reprimand, instead of allowing for the possibility that my mom liked hanging out with me. I didn't want to acknowledge, either, that what I considered to be a punishment was her regular life or to reflect on the fact that treating the tasks of her regular life as a punishment was mean. I wanted to sit at home in a mood until Eleanor texted me. I'd had a dream she sent me an emoji of a bubble, which was somehow very erotic.

Halfway to the grocery store, we pulled into the gas station, which I resented.

"We still have half a tank," I said.

"If you get gas every time you have half a tank, you never run out," my mom countered, even though I knew she frequently let the gauge fall below a quarter.

Then she told me to get out of the car and pump the gas because I needed to know how. She told me to use the industrial vacuum to exorcize all the demon crumbs from the footwells and the spaces between the seat cushions of the car because she didn't want to do it herself. She didn't say I was required to perform these tasks as penance, because she didn't want me to think I only had to be helpful while I was being punished. Still, I felt punished. I pumped the gas and vacuumed the crumbs, and my mood radiated from my body in black waves. I felt ready to cry or throw a glass vase.

By the time we arrived, I was in a complete slump. I hated the grocery store. I never wanted to have to feed myself in the future. Maybe by the time I became an adult, robots would be responsible for picking up rotisserie chickens. Also, maybe Eleanor would never text me ever again. Margaret clearly thought I was an idiot or a baby. I couldn't be counted on to follow her any of the places she wanted to go, any of the places teenagers went when they weren't willing to postpone until college what we referred to as capital E Experiences. Three years of high school remained. I wasn't up for them. I'd made it this far but could no longer remain a cool person.

My mom pressed a hand between my shoulder blades, which in our language meant that I should stand with better posture. That day, it felt like an incitement to ill temper. She never let me forget myself. I felt my mind sharpen. I was about to say something awful, but she quickly withdrew her hand, as though she'd just then remembered how things stood between us, which hurt me too. I didn't really want her to go away. I rolled my eyes and failed to straighten my posture. Through the sliding glass doors, I leaned over our shopping cart, my arms stretched out along its cool metallic rim and my feet dragging behind me. My mom ignored this bad-mood theater. She held peaches up to her face in the produce section.

"You can tell which are good based on how they smell," she said.

"I'm aware," I responded, because she told me the same thing every time she looked at a peach.

My mom didn't like the grocery store either. I sensed the

burden of the million choices that had to be made on behalf of herself and two other people—my father, who didn't understand that saying he had no preference about anything was an abdication of responsibility instead of a convenience, and me, physically present but entirely unhelpful—but I failed to register its gravity. We hadn't mentioned my friends since the fight. Probably she was deciding if she should prevent me from having a sleepover with anyone ever again because I had revealed that even same-sex sleepovers might result in kissing, and parents weren't supposed to encourage the advancement of their children's romantic agendas. We turned the corner into the hallway of dairy products, and I bitterly told myself that my mom's first kiss had probably been when she was thirty, married, and already had a child named Mina who was me.

Midwestern grocery stores are enormous, their shoppers buying to feed a family for a week or more, for a party, for a picnic, for a pantry big enough to merit a door. The aisles of this one were wide, tiled, illuminated by blue-white fluorescence. The cold air of the dairy aisle nipped at my bare arms and legs. My mom always packed a coat in her purse and wore it through the refrigerated areas of the store, which was both genius and embarrassing, the usual mom combination.

She slowly opened a carton of eggs for inspection. I felt my skin grow taut with the desire to get warm. I needed to move, to generate heat, but when my mom ran her index finger gently over each little sloped form, such a reassuring gesture, I felt overcome instead by the sudden need to be reassured. I tucked my head into her neck. I was tall enough by then. I put my hands next to hers on the cart and helped her push it forward.

"Hi," she said.

She pulled out her brown-and-silver braid from within her

quilted jacket. The gold face of her wristwatch flashed beneath her sleeve.

"Margaret won't talk to me," I said in a plaintive voice, because I needed my mom to know something about me in that moment and this was the information I felt capable of communicating. "Not the way we usually do."

I pulled down two packages of lox and a tub of cream cheese.

"She is having a hard time right now. You know that," my mom said.

"She's being normal with Eleanor and everyone else," I countered.

We navigated the cart into the dry- and packaged-goods aisle, where I became briefly distracted by a college-aged girl wearing a tank top through which her nipples were visible. She was talking on the phone while she shopped for instant ramen. Her cart was all beverages.

"We don't have to be anywhere until ten," she said to some person I wanted very badly to see. My mom returned to the cart with oatmeal.

"Your relationship with Margaret is different," she said. "You've been there. You've heard her parents fight."

"So has Bea," I pointed out, but as soon as I said it, I knew how she would reply.

"Bea is family," she said.

In the freezer aisle, we moved with our greatest efficiency, my mom pulling out prepared meals for my dad, who sometimes liked to eat a second dinner in the middle of the night. When we emerged into the warmer climate of the bread, bakery, and deli rotunda, my mom consulted her list. I retrieved a plastic sack of bagels, but she waved me off.

"We'll stop for the better ones on the way home. Eleanor may also understand some of what Margaret is feeling in a different way," she continued.

Though my heart accelerated, I heard no special emphasis on Eleanor's name.

"El's parents aren't divorced. They aren't getting divorced, are they?"

"Oh no, I don't think so. But having all those siblings who are so close to each other in age and so far away from Eleanor—she's living in the wake of a different era of her parents' lives."

I hardly knew what this meant, even in the abstract. My parents seemed to have been exactly the same people the whole time I'd been alive and therefore, presumably, had been those people forever. Eleanor and Margaret both understood what it was like to be only one of a series of considerations that factored into their family's decision-making, whereas I, at the time, had lived continuously at the center of my mom and dad's universe.

"I've never heard them talk to each other that way," I said.

My mom tilted her head to the side while she examined a package of raw meat.

"Even so, kids tend to sense what each other understands," she said.

I didn't like when she talked about me as a member of the group that could be cumulatively characterized as children, but I accepted what she meant.

"I could understand," I said.

"Of course you could," she answered. "But that would mean Margaret would have to explain."

In line at the register, my mom remembered that we needed pickles and sent me on a retrieval mission while she loaded our groceries onto the checkout belt. She always placed items in order of heaviest to most delicate, and she handled each intended purchase gently, with a conspicuous gentleness that today was pointed in the direction of the lanky boy who was bagging our groceries and wearing a baseball hat embroidered with the name of the store, a local chain, as though to inform him that someone considered these objects worthy of care. And even though I ran off to get the pickles, I knew she watched him and possibly smiled at him and attempted to beam into his brain through her feminine precision a fear of his own mother, a fear that spoke in his own mother's voice and said that he shouldn't just drop the peaches into the bag or crush the chips beneath the weight of a bottle of dish soap. I'm sure that he didn't.

JULY CLEARED ITS THROAT, AND THE LAST OF THE EARLY-SUMMER storms stomped their feet. Thursday morning after the Fourth, my mom invited me out for a walk. Great sheets of water had fallen throughout the early hours, downing tree branches and knocking over the potted plants that flanked our front door. Bright green leaves littered the sidewalk, and Amelanchier berries thrown from their branches like bombs stained the concrete a bloody purple. My mom wore her tall black rain boots over stiff straight-legged jeans, her hair loose upon her back.

"I think it's been enough," she said. By which she meant, I could see my friends again. The first thing I felt was alarm. I'd been waiting for this news, but that didn't mean I was ready for it. I didn't know why she'd decided I was. Perhaps she understood that summer days have special length and weight and pitied me. Perhaps she'd grown tired of my sullen dragging about the house. Perhaps she'd noticed my conspicuous reading of classic British literature in the living room and approved of my effort. She didn't explain. She didn't apologize for the way she'd made me feel about Eleanor either, but then I wasn't sure she even understood what she'd done to me those few weeks before. I couldn't explain it myself, and I never managed to hold on to my anger at her tightly enough to prevent it from leaking away.

"Well," she said. "Who are you contacting first, now that you're free?"

I shrugged. I didn't know how either of my friends would receive me, whether or not they'd forgiven me, whether or not they'd even been mad at me or merely annoyed with my talent for conjuring problems from thin air.

"One of them or the other," I said. A lingering instinct to protect my life from her remained.

We walked into the street to avoid a section of the sidewalk guarded by an orange mesh net. Two squares of cement had risen at the center where they met, pushed up by the rising and falling temperatures of winter, and now needed to be repaired.

"I can always insist you stay home for a few more days if you want me to," my mom suggested.

I looked at her in surprise. Sometimes my mom made me feel like a clear glass suit of armor with a big red heart inside. She read in me my feelings at nearly the same pace at which I felt them. This habit that she'd been practicing for the entire length of my life still managed to catch me off guard.

Back home, I called Margaret, no video.

"Is El mad at me?" I asked when she picked up. It was the most direct question I could manage.

"What do you mean?" Margaret responded in the good-natured, inquiring tone of voice she used on people she didn't care about very much.

"Because she's not in trouble," I said. "She didn't get in trouble. She never gets in trouble. You're the one with the real reason to be mad at me." I realized as I said it that this was the right thing to say. "Is your mom still holding it against you?" I asked, and paced across the wood floor of my room. The panels groaned beneath me.

"Only when she can't think of anything else," Margaret answered in a more familiar tone. "El probably just wants you to know that she has the right to be mad at you if she feels like it. Like you did do something she could be mad about."

"Because Eleanor's never done anything anyone could be mad about," I said.

After we hung up, Margaret invited me to Eleanor's house via the group chat. Fifteen minutes later, I biked over. The aftermath of that morning's rainstorm was an unabashedly sunny afternoon. No clouds, no risk of clouds, just July heat like a clarified broth pouring over my shoulders between the intermittent shade of the large elm trees that lined almost every street between my house and Eleanor's. Their branches arced over the roadways, making verdant tunnels through which birdsong and the clanging of machinery rang. All summer long, jackhammers and cement trucks worked on cordoned-off halves of streets, fixing the potholes that pockmarked the pavement. I focused on avoiding them. I promised myself I could be normal. I could be the same as I'd ever been, whoever that was.

I walked my bike up Eleanor's long driveway and into her backyard, following the paved path lined by neat rows of hydrangeas to reach the pool—ovular, with a crisp blue bottom and a row of surrounding lounge chairs, cream-and-black pillows on each and a chest of beige towels rolled neatly into cylinders. Eleanor's house resembled a hotel, all its elements present on purpose.

Her mother, Kim, had been educated as an architect, a career later derailed by the arrival of the first of her children and then eventually transformed into her present occupation as an elegant interior designer for the wealthy Midwest by the time Eleanor was born. The family home functioned as a résumé, their sinks all flanked by scented hand soap and towels that matched the wallpaper.

Eleanor and Margaret were already lounging in their bathing suits, and I knew right away that Margaret must have slept over the night before, though neither of them had said so when they invited me. I hesitated among the plants, not yet noticed, and watched while Margaret handed Eleanor half a lemon, and Eleanor began to squeeze its juice on top of Margaret's head. Margaret's hair was already wet and clung to her neck. Eleanor gave the lemon back to Margaret, and they changed position. Margaret got onto her knees behind Eleanor and squeezed the fruit onto Eleanor's head.

Eleanor's hair could hardly have gotten any lighter, but still she diligently stroked the liquid down through its ends. I felt a vise briefly lock around my breathing. My pulse began to beat between my legs. Lemon juice dripped from her hair, which she wore in a blunt cut just above her shoulders. Her shoulders had been deeply pinked by the sun since the last time I saw her in person, as had her collarbone and the high tops of her cheeks. I had not yet allowed myself to masturbate while thinking about Eleanor, because thinking about Eleanor's body with purpose seemed like a mean thing to do to me. All these years there'd been a distance between us. Now I knew the sensation of its sudden, temporary, exquisite disappearance, and I had to hide that knowing from myself, if I wanted to go on as I had been.

I called out my presence, and my friends in unison stood up to hug me. I didn't kiss Margaret on the cheek, so I wouldn't have to kiss Eleanor. Their bodies smelled like lemons and sweat, but one point of difference immediately occurred to me—that the smell of Margaret's body, however familiar, did not and had never made me want to press my face into her chest and neck.

I pulled my dress up over my head.

"Would you like a lemon?" Eleanor asked.

They'd wrung the one in Margaret's hand to a pulp, but she'd go inside and fetch another for me if I wanted. I shook my head. I couldn't possibly stand there and squeeze lemon juice into my hair in front of her after what I'd felt upon seeing her do the same. I couldn't rub sunscreen into myself either. I'd just have to sit there and burn.

"How's Starter Penis?" I asked Margaret while I arranged myself on my chair.

Eleanor appreciated both my tone after the absence and the fact that I hadn't immediately addressed her. I could tell because she allowed herself, briefly, to look me in the eye. Besides, Margaret never could resist a friendly invitation to assume the role of protagonist.

"He's good," she drawled, propping herself up onto an arm bent at the elbow. "But we're actually calling him Parking Lot now. We feel it's more respectful."

Her wrists and fingers glinted in the sunshine, light reflecting off her bracelets and rings. Some of them leaked green copper from having been worn too many times in the pool. The metal must have been hot in the July sun, but Margaret loved the tan lines that looped like white vines up her hands as a reward for this commitment to appearance.

"Also, apparently he's Olivia's new neighbor," she added after a moment.

"What?" I said.

Margaret explained that his family had recently moved into the house, which she and Eleanor found out when they went over there the night of the Fourth. Other boys had been there too.

Margaret retrieved Eleanor's phone from inside the large, fine-mesh bag beside her chair. The same phone Eleanor had not used to text me. It had a new case, encrusted in rhinestones and deliberately evocative of the ultra-femininity that Eleanor enjoyed both making fun of and embodying. She wore a melon-colored terry-cloth bikini that probably wasn't supposed to get wet. Margaret took her hotness much more seriously. She had on a black bikini made of a bandage-like fabric designed to secure the body into curvature and a pair of sunglasses with miniature lenses.

She held El's phone in front of El's face to unlock it, then held the phone in front of mine to reveal a dark image in a windowless basement with a beaten couch that could have belonged to any house in the Midwest. Margaret, Eleanor in my shirt, Bea, and Olivia sat interspersed with boys I didn't really know but recognized from social media as attractive people who attended a different school in the area. We were all aware of each other like that.

One of the boys from the friend group was missing. He must have been the one to take the picture. Margaret must have asked him. Eleanor hated asking anybody for anything, Bea would have asked Margaret, and Olivia typically let Bea bear the discomfort of being in charge. I wished I could have been there to see Margaret decide that she cared more about having the picture than about pretending she didn't need one. Suspicious red cups were visible on the carpeted basement floor. The photo had been framed to include them.

"But El is refusing to post her content," Margaret said.

"You should have posted it with yours," Eleanor replied.

Eleanor never posted pictures of herself smiling in a line with other people. Though she posed with the group when occasion called for it, she let others use their digital real estate on such generic images. The pictures she posted were most often candid adjacent. She liked to be caught in the act of attractiveness, the image slightly blurred by movement.

Margaret sighed. She couldn't be the one to post a picture including both herself and a boy with whom she was then trying to hook up. It was too forward an indication of interest. But the Fourth was only two days prior, which meant we were still within the acceptable window for Eleanor to post about it.

"What happened to your plan of never speaking to him again?" I asked.

"Well," she said coyly. "We're just texting."

Margaret always phrased things to preserve the maximum possibility of interest.

"And, I mean, like," Eleanor continued in Margaret's inflection, "how were you supposed to know he was your mother's sister's daughter's best friend's new neighbor when you committed to a lifetime of silence?"

Margaret grinned at her. "Exactly. I couldn't have known he was my mother's sister's daughter's best friend's new neighbor when I put his dick in my mouth. So now plans have changed."

I had to laugh at that.

"She hasn't told Bea or anyone about him either," Eleanor said. "She almost gave it away, though."

"No, I didn't."

"You did! She asked him in front of everyone else if he liked going to the mall like nine minutes after they had supposedly just met for no reason, and then the next time we looked at each other we started laughing all deranged."

I could imagine it. "What did he say?" I asked.

Margaret waved the question away. "Everyone started talking

about the next thing. And other than that, I've been very secret agent about the fact that we hooked up." The story was already over. I'd failed to notice its ending.

Margaret lowered her pool chair into its most horizontal setting and shifted to lie down on her stomach before unhooking the back of her bathing suit to tan that expanse of her skin uninterrupted. I wondered if I should do the same, if the sight of my bare back might have any effect on Eleanor.

Kim then made a rare appearance on the rear deck of the house, accompanied by a contractor. The two of them carried clipboards and pointed to various aspects of the house's exterior. She had pure, naturally white hair, horn-rimmed glasses, tiny wrists, and a smile like a pamphlet, crisp and official. I wanted to wear all her silk skirts and heeled boots when I grew up. She waved to us before retreating indoors. Eleanor didn't wave back.

"She's in a bad mood because none of my siblings are coming to her party," Eleanor said. Her parents were throwing an anniversary party in August. Margaret and I had already promised to attend.

In solidarity, Margaret offered, "I slept at my dad's over the weekend." She made a displeased face. "His fridge never has any food, and his bathroom doesn't have a trash can." The lack of a waste receptacle in a bathroom was, we understood, inherently hostile to the presence of a teenage daughter.

But the topic of parents passed quickly. What they really wanted to discuss were their prospects for adventure that night.

"I still can't have sleepovers," I said. My mom had told me before I left.

"We'll probably just end up playing *The Sims* again," Margaret said, to comfort me, supposedly.

I adjusted my pool chair into a state of greater recline and rolled onto my stomach. Without my clothes and prostrate, I felt the full force of the sun's attention, the midday heat of midsummer bearing down upon my body. Sweat welled on my lower back, behind my knees, beneath my breasts, my pores open. A water strider sat watchful on the pool water beside me. Its tiny feet dented the iridescent surface. I closed my eyes for several minutes. When I opened them, I caught Eleanor with her hands in my purse.

"Do you have any good lip gloss?" she asked.

I nodded but turned away rather than watch her touch the gloss to her lips. Still, I heard the doe-foot applicator pucker and sigh as she pulled the wand from the tube. Then she got up and said she wanted something to drink. I turned back toward her when she spoke. Her bikini cut a high V across her butt cheeks, and she adjusted the suit by running the tips of her fingers beneath the edge of the fabric up to her hips before she began walking toward the house. When she opened the back door and entered its dark interior, I spoke to Margaret.

"I feel like a hundred years have passed," I said.

"I know," she replied, and swept her sticky hair from her face.

"I missed you," I said.

"I missed you too," she answered. But nothing eased between us.

In pain, I stood and leapt into the deep end of the pool. The water seemed to reach up and snatch me from the air as I fell. I went slack from the shock of the cold, hung suspended for a second in the chlorinated water. Then I pushed off the paved base and began to swim with my eyes barely open. I kicked into momentum. My hair trailed heavy behind me, long legs propelling me across the bottom of the pool in a few strokes. Half a minute later, I came up heaving. Eleanor stood at the edge of the pool, holding bottles of water.

"They drank, but we didn't," Eleanor said. "Just so you know."

I nodded. Then I pressed my hands onto the lip of the concrete and wriggled my body from the pool like a regular hooked fish.

I HAD, UNTIL THAT POINT, BEEN LYING TO MYSELF ABOUT MY ABILITY to return the two of us to how we'd been before Eleanor kissed me. I couldn't. I'd made it too clear what I wanted, had expressed myself to her too thoroughly and repeatedly, and she hadn't responded. Desire is vulnerability. I wanted to take back what I'd written. I wanted to never tell Eleanor a secret again for the rest of my life, which is no way to be someone's best friend. Somehow, I needed to make more of myself so some of me wouldn't belong to her.

The following Wednesday, we reconvened at Eleanor's house to play *The Sims*. Eleanor and Margaret had apparently been playing the game together, which I found rude, though I had no one to whom to complain. Eleanor's room resembled the rest of the house: lightly colored, in a pristine state of order, air-conditioning on. I knew she resented her mother's insistence on maintaining their home as a public space, but she also liked to open the door and find her room airy and pure, counters spotless and curtains billowing. Sometimes she left a single sweater on the floor in protest but otherwise struggled to violate her own sensibilities, however frustratingly they aligned with her mother's.

Eleanor's massive desktop computer had superior hardware, which allowed for a version of gameplay that was inaccessible on my permanently overheated laptop. Eleanor owned every expansion pack and maintained a robust library of game modifications she'd found online and cut into the game's standard code. As a result, all her Sims had divinely slutty outfits and exaggerated facial features that made them resemble Bratz dolls.

Eleanor sat between us, with control of the mouse and keyboard. Around her neck wound her favorite necklace, a thin silver chain with dangling pendant bubble letters that read *Alone Time*. She hadn't worn it in the days since my return. I'd hung out with both Margaret and Eleanor more than once since the pool, though with neither of them alone. The overt friction of my reentry seemed to have passed, but my previous position in the group remained elusive. More than ever before, I was third.

Margaret and I drew our seats to either side of Eleanor at her desk, wooden chairs we'd carried up from the kitchen. The game began to load. Margaret fidgeted in her chair. The Fourth had raised certain expectations for her. A desirable version of summer had finally presented itself, a repeatable social arrangement. Four girls and four boys, they were perfectly balanced—without me, I didn't fail to observe. They had a basement to hang out in. They had access to alcohol, necessitating exclusivity. They couldn't risk a party, just a select few people sneaking over, and Margaret loved to be among a select few, especially when one of them was the boy whom she wanted to see and who had not explicitly asked her to hang out since the parking lot. But Bea and Olivia apparently preferred the uneven ratio. They'd been hanging out with the boys by themselves, as recently as last night. Bea had posted a selfie of herself and Olivia. The plastic basketball hoop attached to a basement wall in the background signified the masculine presence of people not otherwise visible within the image.

"If she had a picture of them with the boys also in it, she would have posted that instead," I said. Bea and Olivia didn't ask other people for what they wanted, which made them less cool than Margaret in my opinion.

"True," Eleanor said.

She had on hand-me-down burgundy mesh athletic shorts from one of her brothers, hiked way up on her hips with the elastic waistband turned over several times.

"That's what they get for not inviting us." She tucked a leg up into the desk. "Selfies."

The wide rim of her shorts gapped from her thighs, leaving a darkened crescent between the fabric and her body. My eyes dragged on the shadow.

The save file Eleanor and Margaret had made together loaded onto the large, curved screen. Every visible Sim was in some state of physical and emotional distress: one giggling maniacally in a bathtub, another in the midst of a fistfight, and a third urinating on the kitchen floor while she shouted Simish obscenities.

Margaret usually checked out of video games after the fifteen-minute mark. Eleanor and I would play on while she looked at her phone. This wasn't rude of us. You're still allowed, when you're fifteen, to waste your friends' time. But Margaret hadn't excused herself from this game. She'd really been playing. I could see her influence in the packed household, the lingerie as outfits, and the somehow more than usually chaotic character names.

As soon as the game loaded, Eleanor let it play. She didn't pause to assess the situation or provide her Sims with instructions. She preferred to see what would happen if the avatars were left to follow their game-generated inclinations before she started telling them what to do. She also sensed Margaret's mood and so made a cheerful announcement: Margaret's boy had recently sent her a picture of his visible erection inside a pair of sweatpants.

"Well, obviously I need to see that," I said with a degree of enthusiasm meant for Margaret but that I belatedly realized Eleanor might consider hurtful. Then I wished she would.

I eyed the picture Margaret held in front of me for what I hoped was the right amount of time. The sight of the hard line against soft fabric had a nonzero effect on me. Evidence of desire is difficult to witness unscathed. My neck felt hot, and looking at the picture while both Eleanor and Margaret looked at me produced a high hum in my brain. Any arousal in front of them felt like a risk of injury. I removed my gaze from the screen. Eleanor waited for my reaction.

"Boys are fools," I said. "Imagine putting your genitals out into the universe."

But Eleanor didn't seem reassured. If anything, she appeared angry, maybe that I'd implied she might require reassurance.

"I haven't decided what to send back," Margaret said, putting her phone away, and I realized she might have been planning to send him an equivalent image of herself. None of us had any idea how to reverse course from the opinion I'd just expressed, so instead we began to watch the Sims.

One of them was about to give birth, which created an existential problem for her housemates. A household could contain a maximum of eight Sims. When you attempted to add a ninth, the game would prompt you to select one of the existing Sims to move out. Or you could murder someone in advance to make room.

"You want to bring a child into this messed-up world?" I joked, but the thought of a tiny digital baby crying unattended scraped me internally like a fine metal comb.

Eleanor, who always knew when I wasn't really kidding, shot me an irritated look and then began the process of voting someone off the island with Margaret. I didn't try to intervene further. This was Eleanor's house, Eleanor's computer, and Eleanor's game with Margaret. I'd been present for thirty seconds and so far said exclusively the wrong things. They'd probably gotten a Sim pregnant on purpose to facilitate this murder scenario. I wanted to seize the mouse and solve every problem. I wanted to feed all the Sims and tell them to go to sleep. I wanted to get up from this desk and leave.

"I think we should get rid of Pizzarina," Margaret said. "Because she's the least good-looking."

Eleanor shook her head. "We should get rid of the Sim that the other Sims like least."

"No! We can't get rid of Clarissa," Margaret protested.

All eight of them were variously entangled with each other, but Clarissa had a number of thrilling hate courtships underway. She was *Enemies with Benefits* with half the house and therefore too central to its drama to be eliminated.

"You're right," Eleanor agreed. "We need the Sim with the least relationship points total, of either positive or negative value."

She reached for a pencil and paper to start recording each Sim's relationships. I looked at Margaret because I knew that she hated and immediately grew impatient whenever Eleanor tried to implement a systematic approach to a problem, but Margaret didn't look back, and when I returned my eyes to the screen, I had the sinking feeling that Eleanor had just withdrawn her gaze from my face. Only then did I hear her start to scrawl across the paper as she took down numbers. That's how easy it is to wrong someone when you aren't properly talking to them.

Then, while Eleanor was still penciling in and comparing the feelings of eight pretend people, the game came to a decision for her. A purple notification box appeared. Kitten, the Sim who'd been left to her own devices in the bubble bath, had transitioned from *Very Playful* into *Hysterical* and was now in the process of *Dying from Laughter*. The Grim Reaper showed up in the bathroom to mop the floor and collect her soul. Margaret cheered, took pictures, and posted them with the caption: *me*.

"You could restart from your last save," I suggested to Eleanor. "If you want to finish your calculations."

I thought this was a friendly offer, but she gave me a haughty look. Cheat codes to print money or manufacture moods were one thing. She drew a different line.

"It's against the spirit of the game," she replied. "To try to take back what you've done."

I locked eyes briefly with Eleanor's reflection on the screen and pushed my hair over my shoulder, baring the side of my neck in her direction. I wasn't the one who was trying to take back anything.

Bea's picture lit up Margaret's phone, and she left the room to answer the call.

I kept promising myself I'd give up on the Eleanor who'd kissed me, but I only made that promise for the pleasure of imagining I'd be forced to break it. I wanted Eleanor to force me to break it.

"Hi," I mouthed.

In response, she gave me a look of such angry susceptibility—an almost outrage against whatever I might say next, against the corridor I'd attempted to open between us—that I shut my mouth quickly, developed pristine posture, crossed one of my legs over the other, and felt I had no interest in ever taking a risk again in my life.

So when Margaret came back and asked if I could sleep over,

I said no, without even messaging my mom to make sure I still couldn't. When she asked Eleanor, Eleanor said yes, and Margaret started to text. The three of us had finally been invited over to the basement.

"I'm telling Bea we can come," she said. I wondered if she also explained why I couldn't, or if she didn't mention me, or if Bea hadn't in fact included me in the invitation in the first place and Margaret had just been being polite when she asked whether or not I could sleep over.

I stayed long enough to help them choose outfits. Eleanor first, with me and Margaret sitting on the floor. She opened all the drawers in her dresser. Her shirts were organized by color.

"I liked the halter situation," Margaret said about a dress with the face of a Renaissance baby angel printed on its chest that Eleanor kept trying on and then taking off again.

"The halter dress is a mood," I confirmed.

Eleanor shook her head, but I figured she might want to try it on again. In an effort to be helpful, I got up to retrieve the dress from her bed, where she'd folded and then discarded it. She walked farther away from me, so I followed, dress extended. She turned around.

"I said I don't want it," she said.

Then she pushed my hands away with real force. My balance slid backward. I stumbled. Then my body was reacting. I surged forward, slight but with immediate and aggressive purpose, putting my hands on her upper arms and pushing Eleanor back. She had to step her foot to the right to regain her posture.

Only a second had passed. I read shock on Eleanor's face, close and beneath me, and then embarrassment. She turned her head away from mine. Her cheeks colored. We'd caught ourselves in a strangeness that could not be easily dismissed. When had we ever touched each other like that before? And I didn't want it to stop either. I had the urge to get into a fistfight. I wanted her to push me down onto the floor. I wanted more of whatever there was between us, more of whatever it was she seemed determined to withhold.

"What is happening?" Margaret asked. She'd gotten up from the floor and was reaching toward us as though to intervene.

"Nothing," I said. "She doesn't have to wear the dress, obviously."

Eleanor turned to her dresser and closed a drawer.

I said I had to go to the bathroom. I averted my eyes from the family photos that lined the hallways of Eleanor's house as I half-ran, though only a fraction of them actually contained her face. When I got to the bathroom, I cried without letting my breathing change. Then I came back out, and we all left for dinner.

When I got home, my mom asked, "Did you really spend the whole day playing on the computer?"

NEITHER MARGARET NOR ELEANOR VOLUNTEERED any information about what happened with Bea and Olivia after I left, and no one posted anything about it either. For the next week, our group chat was quiet. I could only conclude that the two of them were talking to each other without me, making plans to which they didn't want to invite me, not without assurance first that I wouldn't be allowed to attend. I asked them to go play Putt-Putt, but they declined.

i cant today! family stuff, Margaret texted, which could have been real, except that she didn't offer any alternative availability. Eleanor waited until Margaret had replied and then sent a version of the same. She certainly wasn't going to agree to be alone with me.

I was almost grateful. Every time I saw my friends I seemed to make my life worse. But by the following Wednesday, I couldn't stand the stagnation either. I painted my nails. I paced around my room in my underwear with my hair blown dry. It was so hot outside, my mom had finally capitulated to air-conditioning, and a cool breeze blew through the vent in my ceiling. I tried to make sense of the information I had.

Eleanor was a tightly controlled person and then reckless when circumstance aligned with desire. I knew that. It didn't surprise me that she'd kissed someone without a plan for how to behave afterward. What surprised me was that I was the one she'd kissed. Maybe what she really wanted was to be better friends with Margaret, to supersede our almost-since-birth primacy. I had thought Eleanor valued her remove, but then again, before the last few weeks, I'd never experienced that remove myself. I'd thought she liked to recuse herself from the demands of our higher entanglement, to roll her eyes at our extravagances of intimacy and wear her own outfits and go home early, but now she went home with Margaret, and I walked in circles around my room by myself. I'd thought she felt sufficiently loved by us, but perhaps she had not. I was not, after all, at that moment, feeling sufficiently loved.

Sick with thinking, I threw myself onto my bed and read Ginevra and made use of my hands and blankets. I had my whole brain to fill with thoughts other than Eleanor. I got dressed and went for a long walk. I came home and irritably cleaned my room. I folded my laundry. I emptied all my various bags and backpacks and put away their contents: phone chargers, the clear plastic ziplock bags I used as wallets, each with a couple of dollars, a hair tie, and a lip product. I took my bathing suit out of the side pocket of a large canvas tote bag, the bag I'd brought to Eleanor's pool the week before. I shook out the rest of its contents.

Onto the floor fell a printed picture of Eleanor bare from the ribs up, taken on a disposable camera, lying on the plush carpet of her bedroom floor, one arm partially visible in the corner, her hair a curved line against her jaw, the pink of her nipples hard against my irises. I turned the picture over. The back of the photo stock showed the name of a pharmacy, which meant she'd brought the camera there, waited an hour at least, and then returned to retrieve the developed film from a pharmacy employee. She'd brought the pictures home. She'd waited to see me again. On the first day she saw me after we kissed, she'd hidden this image in my bag. I had her permission to look at it. She'd given the picture to me on purpose, so that I could look at it. That was the only explanation for its presence in my possession. I turned the image over again.

In the picture, her nails were painted with silver glitter. She held her favorite necklace taut in her mouth. Her tongue pressed through the gaps in its letters.

JULY BEGAN TO PREPARE FOR AUGUST. THE BLAZING BLUE DAYS AT the heart of the month took on a weighted-blanket quality toward its end. The wispy white striated clouds of earlier summer gained heft, turned pale silver, and hung daylong in the sky like objects on a mobile, undispersed by the sun. In that weather, we all felt summer's deadline. We looked down the season's golden carpet and saw its tasseled edge. If we were going to turn into other people, we'd better hurry up and do it—which was why Margaret balayaged her hair, dying her dark chestnut waves to fade into honeyed tips.

"Incredible," I said when she turned up at my front door on the last Saturday of the month looking shiny and new. "Genuinely fantastic. A trendsetter. Gorgeous."

"And you look like a sexy tube of toothpaste," she said when she saw my mint-green outfit. I had on white sneakers with an inch of platform and shorts so short the pockets only fit half my phone and two thirds of my butt cheeks. I hoped Eleanor would wonder if my shorts were for her benefit. By which I mean, I hoped Eleanor would take my butt cheeks personally.

We had dressed for the occasion: Every summer, our corner of Ohio offered one of the oldest continuously running agricultural fairs in the country. Or rather, a corner of Ohio adjacent to our own. The fair took place a county away, a good forty-five minutes driving east on the highway, longer if you hit traffic.

My mom disapproved of the great quantities of fried food, creaking metal rides, and general spirit of intoxication, or at least she never had any interest in attending herself. She liked reading books and going to museums. She didn't like trudging around in the heat and having to explain that all carnival games were designed to take away your money. We never went to the fair when I was a child. If we were driving anywhere for entertainment, it would be toward the city and not away from it. I didn't protest, because I hardly knew the fun I wasn't having.

The fair, however, took on a new significance as I got older. All the teenagers who lived within an hour's drive attended, all those various schools with their separate social lives pooling uniquely into one place, making the fair an annual opportunity for plot none of us could stand to miss. A wide wake of photographic output always trailed the event on social media, guaranteeing material for discussion. Obviously, it was better to have pictures of yourself to include in the cumulative online portrait than only to dissect everybody else's.

I'd gone for the first time the previous year, though not very successfully. Eleanor got sick and canceled. Margaret made her plan with Bea before I had a chance to ask—or at least, when I asked, she claimed to have. Bea was a more thrilling person to go with than I was. Bea's mom drove the two of them, a thinly plausible explanation for why Margaret didn't offer me a ride. I met them there. We had fun, but I left before nighttime like a child. A few hours was the longest my mom could tolerate entertaining herself in the area before returning to retrieve me, and she insisted I leave the fair by seven because she didn't like getting home after eight unless it was for her own reasons instead of mine.

On the heels of my broken summer, I determined to do

better. I didn't ask Margaret. Instead I told her, in front of Nancy, who always wanted help with rides, "Mar, my mom can drive us to the fair in the afternoon, if you want."

"Oh, yes," Nancy agreed on Margaret's behalf immediately. "Please thank Celeste for me," she said. "I can pick you girls up at ten." Because unlike my mother, Nancy was an adult who stayed awake after the sun set. Once I'd secured Margaret, Eleanor hardly needed to be asked. She planned to meet us there, her mother having some errand to complete nearby, and all three of us agreed to sleep over at Margaret's house afterward, my first night sleeping in anyone's bed other than my own since the start of summer. Which meant that for the first time in weeks, I was live. I was on the scene as it happened.

My mom drove with a single hand on the wheel, her hair in a neat braid down her back. She sensed the intensity of our desire to have fun radiating from the back seat and so felt called upon to warn us of the various evils she imagined we might encounter. She confirmed we knew not to accept food or especially drinks from people we didn't know, or even people we knew but didn't trust, or who seemed too eager to see us consume whatever they'd provided.

"And don't ride any rides that seem suspicious," she said.

"Suspicious how?" I asked. I didn't like when my mom said things for my benefit in front of other people. Instruction was our private business.

"Like they might fall apart." That was literally all of them.

"What about strangers?" I asked. "Should we get into their vans?"

"Yeah," Margaret joined in. "What about their basements—should we ask to see their basements?" I'd missed Margaret badly.

"No basements," my mom said from the front seat, not trusting us enough for humor. "You girls keep each other safe."

I wedged my hands under my thighs. She thought everyone on earth was my personal responsibility. She didn't know I'd lost my right to order Margaret around.

We got off the highway and drove the last ten minutes through a suburban neighborhood that I recognized as much more likely to host a massive agricultural fair than the one where we lived. Doan shared a county with Cleveland, which we'd now left. The quantity of American flags waving from front porches increased. The houses grew either closer together or noticeably farther apart, with no sidewalks to connect them. Passing through Main Street, we saw a church, a popcorn shop, and a memorial set up on the side of the road.

My mom pulled into the lot next to the fairground. As soon as she put the car into park, Margaret and I rushed out. In the vehicle, we still belonged to my mother, but as soon as the car vanished from sight, we would be no one's. We would just be people in a crowd. Right away, the day's baking heat began to sheen our skin. My mom rolled down her window. Margaret took a few courtesy steps onto the sidewalk while I lingered to say goodbye.

"I can always come back and get you," she said quietly. "Even if Margaret and Eleanor stay."

The implication that I might need rescuing made my face hot. "I know," I said. "Thank you." Then I kissed her on the cheek through the window and turned away.

I grabbed Margaret's hand. We both had on miniature backpacks. We took off at a jog toward the entrance, an enormous balloon archway. A woman wearing a green gingham button-down shirt and a zippered vest with a metal pin with her name on it took our entry fee and stamped our hands. The cost of admission came with an accordion-folded paper guide to the grounds, which I knew I'd keep.

It is lightly thrilling to be handed a map. On the attached schedule: a bulb show, a magic show, a wood-carving demonstration, a hot-air balloon ascension, a demolition derby, and fifty other things I didn't bother reading. The fair wasn't an event you could attend alone. The sheer quantity of people present and physical sprawl of the grounds meant that everyone arrived in an alliance. It served as a reminder of the power of our own, how much better off we were in each other's company, the mutual glow of our shared attractiveness, the safety of our closed unit. Groups of teenage girls scare people for a reason.

"Let's go to the bumper cars," Margaret said.

"What about Eleanor?" I asked.

"El can find us," Margaret announced with what I considered to be unreasonable confidence.

Getting lost at the fair was easy. Uneven aisles containing carnival games broke and twisted into new corridors of sticky food—the smells of cooked meat and burnt sugar often heady, sometimes fading—that wrapped around the fair's largest anchor points, sprawling tents and pavilions housing livestock and produce for exhibition. Massive, dubious metal rides served as compass points because they could be seen from a distance, hulking above the temporary city of red, white, and yellow stands. The fair's full sprawl encompassed almost a hundred and fifty acres of open land, which meant that every year, groups of friends agreed on designated meeting points only to ignore or forget them.

"We can wait five minutes," I countered, and purchased a crushed-ice apple cider for four dollars. I drained the liquid in a few sweet gulps, leaving behind a cup of shaved ice, no juice.

"Do I need to throw this at you?" I asked Margaret because of the impatient look on her face. She laughed and held her own cup of ice to her neck.

Our phones vibrated simultaneously with a message from Eleanor. It was a picture of ourselves in the crowd. I looked tall and tan against my minty clothes. Margaret had one hand on her hip, her brown-to-blond hair visible even from a distance.

"She's so good at taking those," Margaret said, in an almost resigned tone of voice, because Eleanor mostly took pictures when she felt like it, which was not as often as Margaret would have liked. "I swear this will be the best photo of me all day."

I turned in the direction from which the photo had been taken and saw Eleanor skipping toward us in a matching set, brown oval tortoiseshell sunglasses, and a miniature backpack.

"M and M together again," Eleanor said, which for a moment felt pointed to me, but then she kissed each of us on the cheek, Margaret and then me, her face against mine so briefly, her Alone Time necklace dangling from her neck.

It occurred to me that in all the days since giving me the picture of herself, El couldn't have known whether or not I'd seen it and therefore hadn't had to act as though she'd sent it. Unlike me, at the pool, looking at her phone in her hand and knowing that she'd read all my messages and answered none of them. All I had to do was the same: Be regular. In my favor, Eleanor was distracted. She loved the fair. It was full of games and animals and dirt. She wanted to see the animals first.

"I'm not here to visit livestock," Margaret countered.

I pointed out that if we didn't see them first, we'd have to see them later.

The tents smelled of hay and animal bodies, warm, alive, and somehow private. The one thing El wasn't allowed was a pet in the house, and her face softened to see the alpacas with their fuzzy Q-tip heads and the baby cows blinking their long, cartoon lashes. Margaret, once she got there, volunteered to feed a horse some hay and giggled when she felt the mare's hot breath on her palm.

"Mina is reading informational placards because obviously," Eleanor said when she saw me standing next to a sign that explained the fair's numerous competitions. She knew I loved an explanation. Prizes had already been awarded to the roosters for their crowing, the chickens for their flying, the goats for their dairy, and the piglets for their ability to run around a track. Eleanor's awareness of me made my chest rise. I reminded myself again that she didn't know I'd seen the picture and she didn't know either for how long I'd looked. Then again, when had I ever been able to hide anything? My heart beat in my throat.

"In case you were wondering, this one is a champion," I said, and pointed to a piglet who was then taking a nap next to its mother, milk around its mouth.

El walked over to stand beside me in front of the wooden enclosure. I leaned my arms against the top of the wall, and she leaned as well. The length of her hair now touched her shoulders. Its strands slid across my arm when she moved.

"That's the right way to behave as a champion," she said. "Take a nap." She pulled her phone in its sparkling case from her pocket to take a picture of the piglet. Then she flipped to the front-facing camera. In the screen, we both saw Margaret behind us and then turned around to look. She had positioned herself near the exit. She was acting busy on her phone while occasionally scanning passersby on the off chance any of them wanted to fall in love with her. She had rearranged her shirt to be shorter.

Eleanor rolled her eyes briefly, just the slightest rise of

her dark pupils into her mascaraed eyelashes, which made me shiver—the pleasure of being included, the pleasure of observing her mood. "Come be in this," she called to Margaret, and then handed her phone to me because I had the longer arms. Eleanor and I tilted our heads toward each other. Margaret posed behind us, one arm in the air and a hip out. Eleanor and I separated to make room for her in the space between our faces.

Our tour of fauna concluded in the rabbit pavilion, a cavernous space with a ceiling supported by enormous wooden beams. Great long rows of folding tables ran up and down the room, each row holding something like fifty cages, each one with its own upside-down water-bottle dispenser suspended over a bed of shaved wood. The heady smell of alfalfa permeated the enclosure.

Eleanor walked slowly from cage to cage, making long eye contact with each rabbit who was willing. I saw her mouth moving. She spoke to them softly, possibly on the topic of their ears, which looked soft enough to create a pained sensation in my chest, or perhaps that was Eleanor and the unguarded tenderness that swept like rare weather across her face.

Margaret finished inspecting rabbits in a few minutes. I saw her idling by the door, scanning the crowd of pedestrians.

"It's too hot out there," I said by way of persuasion. The shady pavilion was a relief from the afternoon's dusty heat.

Then Eleanor stepped into the long line of people waiting to hold the designated patting rabbit. Margaret watched, waiting for Eleanor to glance toward us in consultation or make some gesture of acknowledgment, but El only looked at the bunny, who was then being caressed by a seven-year-old. Everyone else in line was either a parent or a child. Margaret, I knew, disapproved of aligning ourselves with ages we'd too recently been.

"Eleanor is literally an infant," she said with an edge in her voice.

I shook my head. "She just likes people less than you do."

"She likes rabbits more than she likes us."

"No, she likes rabbits more than she likes people other than us."

Margaret rolled her eyes—a petting zoo would not advance the plot, in her opinion—and told me she had to go to the bathroom.

Before walking away, she said, "Stay here and make sure Eleanor doesn't wander off after a lamb." This possibility was as likely as Margaret wandering off on her way to or from the bathroom because she ran into a girl she met at some camp three years ago or a boy in the middle of a growth spurt. I joined Eleanor in the line, which ran down the middle of the pavilion, some ten or twelve kids ahead of us, rows of rabbits alongside. She fanned herself with her folded map, face shining with perspiration.

"We could have gone with her if she'd waited five minutes," Eleanor said, irritated.

We were alone. Because I knew something she didn't, I felt it was my turn to move us forward. I had to proceed cautiously. As soon as Eleanor sensed that someone thought they had a right to a certain kind of behavior from her, she rescinded all generosity. She gave freely or not at all. Uncertain, I said nothing. Bunnies rustled in their cages around us, chewing alfalfa, grooming their friends. I felt too tall. I felt an unfortunate desire to lay my cheek on top of Eleanor's head. My body told me this was a thing I could do. My body told me I could wrap my arms around her shoulders and rest my cheek atop the part in her hair. I told my body to please shut up.

When we got to the front of the line, Eleanor confidently

lifted the large rabbit from the arms of the fair attendant. His coat was a wonderful cinnamon color. His impossibly fat neck formed a plush ring of fur into which he could rest his face, like an airplane pillow. El stroked him contentedly and without hurry, in spite of the shifting line of children behind us. Not all of them would get to hold the bunny before the attendant retired him from duty. Rabbits could only withstand a fixed quantity of attention before demanding retreat. Eleanor felt a kinship.

I marveled at her frictionless surface, the way the world slid across her skin without sticking. The tense energy of the line behind us grated on me. I resisted the impulse to tell her to hurry up and scratched the soft space above the bunny's brow, between his ears, felt him watching me with wary pleasure and felt El watching me too, the rabbit in her arms.

"I'd let you poop all over my house," she said to him, even though I knew she wouldn't have. She returned the bunny to the attendant reluctantly when her time was up. Then she tried to get in line again, but Margaret returned from the bathroom and led us away from the pavilion into the aisles of the fair.

Margaret strutted a few feet in front of me and Eleanor like a marching-band conductor. Her hair bounced on her back. She wanted to maximize our surface area. The fair represented an opportunity to engage with people who we could usually only observe online. Normal rules of communication didn't apply. If you saw someone at the fair, it was considered reasonable to send them a message even if you hadn't talked to them, which meant there was additional value in being seen. Margaret wanted to open as many avenues of interaction as possible. I was fine to follow, but El kept stopping to examine carnival game prizes, goldfish in knotted plastic bags, cans of Silly String, cups of slime, and multitiered tiaras. Her mother's good taste forbade the presence of junk, so Eleanor couldn't help yearning after the colorful flotsam that oozed from every tent and stand.

"Wouldn't it be fun to have an enormous bear?" she said to me, which I found very endearing, but Margaret showed no signs of slowing down. I caught up and touched her shoulder.

"Let El play games," I said. "It's too early for all this running around. Everybody here is still a five-year-old. We'll see people later."

"Sure," Margaret said. "A game couldn't hurt."

We all heard the singular. Eleanor gave Margaret a look that meant, *Other people also have favorite parts of going to the fair*. Margaret merely walked toward the nearest tent. We followed, and Eleanor lost five dollars throwing a ball at a bunch of bottles designed to never fall over. She wanted to try again. She'd looked up strategies for beating carnival games ahead of time and was determined to triumph. Margaret sighed, removed her miniature backpack, and began to adjust its straps. She gave me a look that meant, *Eleanor is being very Eleanor*.

Bumper cars temporarily restored the peace, as both my friends loved violently banging into each other and strangers while screaming. Then mini golf, which presented the opportunity of taking pictures of ourselves half bent over. Eleanor won. Then we finally began to see people we knew and flung our arms around their necks and impressed them with our outfits, and Margaret built her way toward six different evenings, making vague but exclamatory promises, telling people we'd meet them at a ride later but not what time.

She wouldn't let us linger with any of these groups for long, lest they think we belonged to them, cutting us off from alternatives. She surged ahead through a crowd of strollers and dented clouds of cotton candy, ducking and weaving through the gaps between shoulders, propelled by her infinite store of energy and the sight of the back of some tall boy's head. She paused periodically for us to catch up, but once we did, she'd take off again.

Eleanor kept getting bumped and jostled by the other fairgoers. She had to stop and get out of the way, slowing her down. She was much smaller than I was and had less of an I'm-coming-through vibe than Margaret. Eventually, I offered to carry her on my back. Her chest pushed into my shoulders. Her legs wound around my waist. I felt her hesitate to position her face beside mine. Instead, she rested her cheek against the back of my neck. Her cheek was hot.

Five minutes later, we reached the fair's eastern edge to find a spectacular regiment of farming equipment. I set Eleanor down. Neither of us looked at the other. Even the possibility of eye contact felt explicit so soon after having her pressed against me. A hundred or more shining tractors stood in neat rows before us. Fathers helped their kids up into the hot black seats so they could pretend to drive. Margaret gave her phone to Eleanor and grabbed my hand, pulling me up onto a green-and-yellow machine.

We wrapped our arms around each other and smiled with our cheeks smushed. She stood and I sat. I sat and she stood. I had been absent from the majority of Margaret and Eleanor's documentation of that summer and felt determined to get a good picture. But Eleanor was doing the job unenthusiastically. She looked impatient. She wasn't pushing the button on Margaret's phone often enough to capture the in-between images we admired. Nor did she shout any compliments, provide instructions, or even make any encouraging noises to dissipate the awkwardness of publicly posing for a photo.

In the absence of vocal encouragement, I began to feel we were doing something wrong. Around us, adult men spoke with salespeople and leafed through brochures about equipment. A few of them idly observed our posing, looked away. These machines were being sold and would eventually make incisions in the earth. We'd positioned ourselves among the instruments of a life different than our own and used them as props. The rules of my world with Margaret and Eleanor had fractured over the course of the summer, rules that helped to insulate me from larger social norms and the anxieties of imagining how I might be perceived, as a very tall young girl from an affluent suburb posing on a tractor with her butt cheeks out—things I didn't want to matter. I felt momentarily lonely and dumb and climbed down.

"Thank you!" I called out in the direction of the saleswoman. She didn't look up from her clipboard. As I dismounted, I saw a group of girls waiting to take our place. They set their drinks down on the ground and adjusted their hair. Margaret realized she knew them and began an enthusiastic hello process without getting down from the tractor. Instead, she waited for one of them to climb up with her and began a new round of photo taking, conducted by another of the girls. Since I wasn't needed and not in the mood to be introduced, I walked over to Eleanor and noticed that she didn't look well. Her cheeks and forehead were flushed, her posture slumped. The many hours of heat had become too much for her, the crowds, the constant walking.

"Are you okay?" I asked quietly, standing with my back to the tractor, so Eleanor would know the question was private. "Let me get you some water."

I paid at a food stand while she waited nearby, not wanting to get into line herself.

"It's a million degrees outside," she explained.

I nodded, used to being the member of the group who was having a problem and wanting to shield Eleanor from the feeling. The bottles were soaking wet, just pulled from a cooler full of ice. The plastic was so thin they crinkled, bent, and folded as we drank. Eleanor spilled water down her chin and onto her chest. I got her a napkin. Around us, families were beginning to file out of the fair, their children sticky and tired. The crowds of people our own age thinned out too as everyone retreated to houses for dinner and an hour or two of rest before returning for the evening.

"Let's find a place to sit down," I said, and when she didn't immediately decline, I turned to tell Margaret, who remained atop the tractor, supremely visible, chatting away, that it was time for us to leave, but Eleanor grabbed my wrist, hard. Then, noticing the strength of her grip, she let go.

"We're going to lose Margaret when Bea and Olivia get here later, anyway," she said with an outright annoyance that caught my attention. Usually, I was the one who complained about Margaret to Eleanor, and Eleanor was the one who reminded me to let Margaret be who she was. Also, complaints about a third person were an invitation to confederacy, and Eleanor hadn't openly invited me to anything in weeks.

"Fair," I said. The knit of afternoon clouds temporarily loosened, and the sun punched through. I led Eleanor into a patch of shade.

"Why is it so easy for you to do what she wants?" she asked.

I gave her a look of incredulity. I could rarely do what Margaret wanted. I'd had to negotiate with my mother just to attend the event where we then stood.

"I don't mean logistically," she clarified. "I mean in general."

"I don't when it's only the two or three of us," I said, a little defensive. Did Eleanor not see me as a person who held her own?

"Isn't it worse when it's in front of other people?"

I shifted my weight from one leg to the other. These questions held an accusatory edge I didn't understand, but at least, at last, for a moment, Eleanor seemed to be speaking to me frankly. My pulse sped.

"I guess I feel like she has my permission. Like I want her to—under certain circumstances."

Eleanor's eyebrows, so blond they were almost invisible, furrowed. "What are the circumstances?" She truly wanted to understand. Something about her own relationship with Margaret had gone off-kilter, and she'd come to consult me on mine.

"I also tell her what to do," I said, which was more a defense of myself than an answer to the question she had asked. The circumstances in which I wanted to be led were when I liked Margaret's leadership.

"She's not in charge of us," Eleanor said fiercely.

Did she want me to like Margaret less?

"She's not in charge of us, but it's usually more fun if we let her be," I answered. Eleanor and I both knew that from experience. We knew we benefited from what Margaret did for us, on our behalf, and therefore spared us from having to do. The preliminary gestures, the establishing tone. If Margaret drove the car of her charisma, we got to sit prettily in its back seat.

But maybe Eleanor didn't want me to explain the advantages of our usual division of social labor with Margaret. All our usual divisions were off, warped, and had been since she kissed me. She smoothed the sweaty baby hairs from her face and tucked them behind her ears.

"I can't be how the two of you are," she said.

"How are we?" I asked.

"You know how."

I did know. I knew what Margaret and I were usually like, and I understood what Eleanor wanted me to acknowledge.

"But we're not like that right now," I said. "We haven't been like that for weeks."

Eleanor had been Margaret's best friend, not me. She knew that, and yet she wanted me to say it aloud. My face burned from acknowledging what I'd lost. Eleanor's eyes looked both green and gray, a little bit triumphant, like she wanted me to say more, but then she looked over my shoulder, which meant Margaret was coming. The clouds reknit overhead, sealing off the light.

"I want to eat a cheeseburger," Margaret said, skipping into our midst. "Let's go eat cheeseburgers." The girls she'd been talking to were driving to a nearby fast-food chain to meet up with their guy friends, but they only had one remaining free seat in the car.

Eleanor refused to follow on foot. "Can't we sit under a tree or something?" she asked.

"Yeah," Margaret answered. "We could definitely chill for a couple of minutes and regroup before we walk over." I was going to have to tell her to cut it out with this phrasing. "Mina, what do you want to do?" she asked.

Eleanor looked at me too for my answer. They both wanted me to intervene. For the first time since the start of summer, I was between my friends instead of outside them, but not because they both wanted to hang out with me. Rather because I was the third vote. I was the most likely conduit for either of them getting what they wanted out of the next few hours, a position I didn't enjoy, to say nothing of how little it made me feel loved.

Another possibility for the evening existed. I could remain behind with Eleanor while Margaret went with the other group, and we could reconvene later. This solution had obviously occurred to Margaret. I could tell—I saw her smile over at the other girls, still standing by the tractor, waiting for her answer—and I was offended by it. If we separated, there was no guarantee we'd find Margaret again. She'd return to us only when the fun of the other group ran out. We were supposed to be hanging out the three of us. On the other hand, Eleanor and I could be alone together for hours. I think this occurred to Eleanor too, because when I looked over to gauge her reaction, she was rapidly typing on her phone. Margaret proceeded without my encouragement.

"Unless you guys want to hang here?" she said, raising her voice up into a question. "And I could meet you in like an hour or two, whenever everyone starts to show up again." Margaret, I thought, wanted to investigate what it would be like to have friends who weren't us.

"Actually," Eleanor announced, "I'm leaving. I have a ride." Apparently her mom was still in the area.

"Wait, are you sure?" I asked, confused and bereft. What was she doing?

"Yeah, are you sure?" Margaret echoed in a way that made my question sound hollow because hers was. I couldn't decide if Margaret was more relieved to get rid of an impediment to her plans or annoyed because without Eleanor she couldn't also leave me. I wanted to whack her in the head.

"I'll come with you," I said to Eleanor. "Do you want me to come with you?" She declined. I asked again, in case the no was perfunctory. "I can come with you." Surely after all we'd just said, she'd rather hang out with me than leave me with Margaret. But in fact, after all we'd just said, she wanted to be alone. She'd engaged her solitude protocol and wanted to get away as fast as possible.

"No," she said. "I want to go back." She hugged me goodbye with a great deal of air between our bodies and then walked off into the crowd without turning around for one last wave. I waited, in case, but after a minute she disappeared from view, and a heavy, empty feeling spread through my stomach.

"She always does this," Margaret said, as though neither of us had had anything to do with her leaving.

I didn't want to walk a mile in the heat to reach a cheeseburger I could have bought fifteen feet from where I was standing. Yes, I felt bad for having indicated I'd be willing to follow Eleanor into leaving Margaret, but on the other hand, Margaret had at the time been in the middle of indicating that she wanted to leave me and Eleanor both. Margaret and I knew we could be mad at each other for these offenses, or we could allow them to cancel each other out in favor of preserving the possibility of a good time. I'd hardly been eligible for a good time all summer, and Margaret prided herself on her resilience of spirit with respect to socializing, so we walked twenty-five minutes down the sidewalk of a multi-lane commercial boulevard fed by highway exits, dripping with sweat, to arrive and find that the girls hadn't come. We had to start laughing.

"If El were here," I said as I got into line, "she would have bought a large cup of soda and then thrown it at us."

Margaret bent over and put her hands on her knees theatrically to catch her breath. "She would have cut off all my fingers and toes."

The vibe in the restaurant was almost hilariously grim, most of the tables empty, their chairs askew, a giant line of cars around the building waiting for the drive-through because none of the drivers wanted to come inside. We had no reason to be there and none to ever come back again. Other locations of the same chain existed closer to home, making the dinner a strange and unique event. Most places in our lives we went to either routinely or on vacation. To be somewhere we'd brought ourselves, not driven by our parents, a place both unknown and unremarkable, highlighted the arbitrariness of our life's container, which made us laugh even more.

"This is like the world's most random place we could be right now," I said.

We looked at each other and shook our heads. We ate our food in a booth. Margaret took off all her rings before she touched her fries. Our phones lit up simultaneously. Eleanor had tagged us in a photo from the animal pavilion. She'd taken the picture without telling us. In the left foreground, her face in profile. In the right background, myself and Margaret with our backs to the camera, leaning over a wooden fence, my butt cheeks slightly visible beneath my shorts and Margaret's new hair down her back in smooth waves. Beyond the fence, I knew, were some cute pigs. The caption read. *incognito mode*.

"Holy shit, she loves to be inscrutable," I said.

"Loves it," Margaret said. "I mean, she's good at it. Her pictures never look like anyone else's."

"She knows at least one of us will post something normal, so she doesn't have to. I'm going to post a picture of your nostrils instead."

Margaret laughed. "Please do," she said. "Please do because then that's what we'll be. One of El's inexplicably sexual candid photographs for the internet and a picture of my nostrils."

The memory of Eleanor's very explicably sexual posed

photograph for me flashed like a lightbulb in my brain and then faded to black just as quickly, the image too corrosive to my social normality to linger.

"That is who we are." I grinned, one third of a cheeseburger stuffed in my cheek. "Just those two things."

Margaret finished her fries and wiped her fingers one by one on a brown paper napkin before putting back on her rings. All her rings, necklaces, and most of her bracelets were delicate metal. Thin chains and fine charms that she copiously layered. She had one real gold necklace, a gift from her parents when they told her they were separating, with a small butterfly pendant, which she wore every day. All the other pieces had to be cycled in and out as their metal coating wore away, sometimes staining her skin.

"You know, El also left like this when we went to Olivia's," Margaret said as she removed the ring that she'd slid onto her right ring finger to try it on the other hand. "She didn't sleep over."

I wondered if Margaret knew Eleanor was mad at her. Eleanor leaving a function on her own inconvenient schedule was normal enough, but the questions she'd asked me hadn't been.

"Did she say why?"

Margaret considered the question. "No. She said she wanted to sleep at home. I had to make up a family emergency to explain why she suddenly bounced. Like, she's not their friend. She's my friend who I brought with me to Olivia's house."

Eleanor leaving would have been less significant if I'd been there, but I hadn't. I repositioned myself at the table, sat with my back against the inner corner of the booth and my legs sprawled over the cushion. Knowing Margaret had been thrust into a weird social situation as a result of my absence improved my mood. Knowing something about Eleanor that Margaret apparently didn't made me downright cheerful. I'd been the one to know the least for weeks.

"Were they bothered?"

"Not really."

"But they could have been."

"They definitely could have been."

I remembered to text my mom confirmation of my continued well-being.

"Do you think El's mad I didn't leave with her tonight?" I asked.

"I mean, she can't be."

This stung a little. I wanted Eleanor to demand I leave places when she left and feel sad if I didn't. On the other hand, Margaret's expression had opened in response to the question. She rearranged her jewelry in the way that meant she was present. The confederacy I'd felt with Eleanor talking about Margaret, I now felt with Margaret talking about Eleanor. The confederacy was the same and not the same. In both cases, talking about the girl who wasn't there seemed like the only way of saying something true.

"Are you mad I offered? I didn't want to like abandon you, but she seemed—"

"I know. It's okay. Obviously, she wasn't going to say yes when you offered anyway."

"I don't like being between the two of you," I said.

"I don't like being between the two of you either," she said.

A child in line for food wailed briefly about the absence of a blanket.

"Is El ever between the two of us?" I asked. By which I meant, had she been between us in the time since she'd kissed me, the time of the loneliest summer in my short and urgent teenaged memory, the only summer I'd not spent almost every day of which with Margaret? Had Eleanor been between us while Margaret spent those weeks with people she had historically liked less than me but that I now worried she liked more, even if she still loved me, even if I believed our love was written in too permanent a marker to be so easily wiped away?

Margaret studied me. I felt like I hadn't had her full attention in years. I felt like she hadn't looked me all the way in the eye since June, which was strange. It seemed especially strange now that we were talking like this. Having a conversation we'd never had before still felt more normal than the way we'd been acting, because it was revelatory, and we were usually always revealing things to each other.

"She must be sometimes, if the three of us are really equals to each other," Margaret answered.

I wondered if we were equals and what even was the nature of the measure.

After dinner, queasy from meat and shriveled by air-conditioning, we retreated to the bathroom to fix ourselves. A damp chemical aroma clung to the room, which was windowless and wet. It had been recently serviced. Large gray squares tiled the floor, and brown sheets of metal enclosed the few stalls.

Our faces confronted us in the twin mirrors above the two sink basins. We appeared melted. Our skin shone through our makeup. Our hair, curled and matted from the heat, stuck to our temples and fuzzed from our foreheads. We stood for a moment disoriented by the work of retroactively pasting the faces we saw in the mirrors onto the way we'd thought we looked in our memories of the immediate past. We'd chosen all our gestures and actions in part because of how we imagined ourselves to look while performing them. We'd imagined wrong.

"Well," I said, "alright," extending one hand out in front of me, as though holding off unwelcome input. Margaret caught my eye through the mirror, and we started cackling. This was exactly why I tried not to check photos as I took or had them taken of me. I tried to wait until the night was over in case my face was going to hurt my feelings.

"Okay, but the lighting in here is terrible," she said. "And we just walked a mile. We didn't actually look like this all day."

"What happens when we walk the mile back?" I asked.

"Nothing," Margaret answered. "We become more beautiful."

I giggled, giddy, because we were becoming silly and defiant for each other, the way she always made me. "Right," I said. Then, "The new hair is perfect, though," because it still was, sweaty or not.

Margaret thanked me and started playing exuberantly feminine pop music on her phone. I used a stiff sheaf of ripped brown paper towel to wipe down the bathroom's laminate countertop. We emptied the cosmetic contents of our tiny backpacks onto its surface between the sinks. We washed and dried our faces and armpits, reapplied our makeup, and attempted to desiccate our sweaty scalps by standing beneath the hot, stale-smelling air of the hand dryer affixed to the bathroom wall.

After fifteen minutes of peaceful working, a woman entered wearing pink-and-silver running shoes and a pronged headband. She looked at us as though we were monsters. Margaret turned off our music as a concession, but the result was that the three of us all had to listen to her pee. We moved out of the way while she washed up, a gesture that failed to compensate for us having taken up more than our share of public space. She tried to use soap, but the dispenser had run out. She wrung her wet hands, flinging drops of water onto me and Margaret, then wiped them on her jeans rather than using the hand dryer. She did so with a displeasure pointed in our direction, as though we'd left her with no other option than such base compromises.

"Have a wonderful evening!" Margaret called at the last second, when the woman had already passed almost entirely through the bathroom door, so she had no opportunity to react.

"Lol!" I said.

"L-O-fucking-L," Margaret echoed.

NIGHTTIME ALTERED THE FAIR'S COMPOSITION. ADULTS AND ANImals went home. Young people crushed into the fistful of aisles that remained open past eight, their giddy shrieks and shouts of recognition punctuating the steady mechanical aching of the metal rides. Vendors flooded the air with the smell of cooked sugar. Floodlights beamed blue-gray over the grounds, their faces like electric flowers blooming against the night. The sky faded to pale purple without anyone noticing. A thousand people our own age moved up and down the aisles, looking at each other. We found this mutual appraisal intoxicating.

"Bea fully hasn't texted me back," Margaret said. "She knows we're here."

I rolled my eyes. "Whatever! Stop waiting for someone else to make this fun. It's already fun."

Margaret nodded. "You're right," she said, and we tossed our hair a little.

The most efficient route from the fair's entrance to its point of apex nighttime activity cut through a narrow aisle of square white tents. Each of them belonged to a local business attempting to attract attention from the passing crowds. Beyond the alley of tents on either side, carnival rides loomed like massive neon insects.

The two of us both were and weren't potential customers. We didn't own houses. We couldn't commission custom closets or backyard pizza ovens. We had no money, but we were associated with money that belonged to people who loved us. This tenuous connection still sufficed for businesses to produce trash merchandise that might theoretically be appreciated by our demographic, like small foam footballs and elastic wristbands. As though our parents might see a branded key chain and decide to build a pool in their backyard.

I hated situations like this, scenarios that made half a claim on me as a party to a potential commercial exchange. You have to behave in a certain way once you're someone who could buy something. Margaret might have walked up to any of these booths, given them a fake name, and pretended to be in the market for a new orthodontist for the sake of laughing at being treated as a customer. But I couldn't play games like that, and Margaret knew I didn't like to, so instead she held my hand and walked right through the narrow passageway without allowing for even the possibility of eye contact so that I didn't have to either.

I felt the part of my personality that existed uniquely in the expression of my friendship with Margaret unfurling, and I felt her experience the same. An additional layer of confidence threaded her step, the way she held her neck, my belief in her eliciting and propelling her shiniest self. I'd missed so badly the people we got to be when we were together like this, the feeling of our tiny federation and the resulting conviction that almost every single thing about being alive was ridiculous and we had merely to point it out to each other to laugh. Energy pinged through me. Still holding her hand, I bounded a few steps farther in the direction of the fair's central landmark.

"Come on," I said.

On the Ferris wheel, we rose and fell. Margaret swung her legs hard back and forth, screaming in gleeful horror as the car rocked. I gripped the handlebar giddily and shouted at her to hold still, please God. We sat pressed into each other at the center of the bench and took pictures of our faces in the dark, cheek to cheek, the state of our appearance conveniently obscured by the brilliant and illuminated background.

Below us, we saw people we knew but no one worth risking the perfection of our shared mood, so when we disembarked, we sped through the fair, hugging, saying hello and exchanging sartorial compliments, but then acting as though we had a place to be next and therefore had to take off after only a few minutes of talking. The two of us were like a pair of thieves, a little breathless, knowing the mood we'd entered could only be sustained by an unbroken sequence of action. We had to keep consuming the world if we wanted to keep living in it.

MARGARET AND I SAW BEA and Olivia at the same time. They were standing in the very long line for the Big Loop, a rickety roller coaster that perfectly exemplified my mother's concerns; when its twelve-passenger car reached peak looping speed, the entire metal donut vibrated. Bea stood with one arm wound around Olivia's waist and Olivia with her head on Bea's shoulder. Neither of them was wearing a whole shirt, Olivia in a shrunken tank top and Bea in a long-sleeved men's shirt she'd scissored off at the rib cage with a visible bralette underneath. Olivia had Bea's same impeccable stomach muscles. The two of them liked to go work out together in full hair and makeup and then buy smoothies.

I didn't want to give up being alone with Margaret, but I knew she wouldn't be satisfied with the night unless it meaningfully involved people other than me. She sped over in their direction, calling out her greeting. I followed. A girl three or four back loudly complained about *some people* who thought they could *cut lines*. I flinched. I didn't even like roller coasters. Eleanor didn't either. She didn't like being shot through space by another person. However, she would have ridden any ride if she could have been the one to press the button.

"Mina! Oh my God, hi!" Bea exclaimed as she hugged me. We all immediately took a picture together, though only in one pose. "My phone has like no service here," Bea said. But the different versions of the picture, which she soon after sent me, all went through right away.

I stopped feeling bad about cutting the line when I realized the line was constantly being cut. Every five minutes new people were showing up next to their friends or leaving the line altogether because they saw someone they knew. Part of the reason to ride the roller coaster was to hang out in line, since the line was in the most populous part of the fair, and the event didn't otherwise allow for stagnation. None of us complained when, after twenty minutes, we noticed that we'd hardly gotten any closer to the contraption itself.

Bea only spent one sentence complimenting Margaret's new hair, which I considered insufficient. Her balayage managed to be both a genuine manifestation of her personal style and in complete alignment with what was just right then becoming cool. It deserved to be celebrated as an accomplishment. Bea was probably annoyed that Margaret had gotten balayage first because now that she had, Bea couldn't also get it. Margaret, being younger, could sometimes copy Bea, but Bea could never copy Margaret.

Olivia, while actively talking to us, was also extremely on her phone, engaged in what seemed to be a full-on texting conversation, though the intervals between messages were obviously longer than she would have liked. She kept her phone in her hand, and I saw her check the lock screen and then lower the device to her side more than once. I briefly speculated about the identity of the person keeping her waiting. I thought with great pleasure about how Margaret and I were going to go home, get into bed, and talk about every single thing that every single person had said and done. I stored up details in preparation.

"So where are all these boys I've never met?" I asked because I knew Margaret wanted to know.

Apparently, they'd all gotten too drunk ahead of time and decided to remain in their basement and hang out only with each other instead of coming to the fair, a real misalignment of priorities.

"I swear I don't even know what they do when they're alone. It's not like they ever talk about anything," Bea said.

"Maybe they're all watching porn together," Margaret suggested.

But Bea and Olivia weren't in the mood to be titillated. They were annoyed, indignant that the boys hadn't cared enough about their public efforts of hotness to show up in person, and they were bound to each other by the specific circumstances of their disappointment. They didn't really want to hang out with us or anyone else. They kept looking at each other and blinking.

"Well, where's El?" Olivia said. Margaret rolled her eyes, and Bea looked at me because I was usually the one willing to explain the behavior of my friends.

"Are Mar and El still being weird because they kissed?" Bea asked.

That was what she asked me: if Margaret and Eleanor were still being weird because they kissed. I felt my blood stamping through the veins of my face.

"You're so dramatic," Margaret said to Bea.

My expression must have visibly demanded explanation because, after several seconds in which Bea looked at Margaret and Margaret said nothing further, Olivia explained. Apparently, they'd all played Truth or Dare on the night Eleanor left early. Truth or Dare was merely a means of forcing specific events to transpire. One of the boys dared Olivia to kiss her neighbor, the boy Margaret was pretending she didn't like. Then he dared Margaret to kiss Eleanor, which she did. Then Margaret dared Bea to kiss Olivia. Then Olivia dared Bea to kiss another of the boys and so on. None of the boys kissed each other. I knew without having to ask that none of the boys had kissed each other. Only girls kissed each other for the benefit of other people.

"Basically, everybody made out with everybody," Margaret capped the explanation, raising a million more terrible questions I couldn't ask.

I noticed I wasn't breathing properly. Short shallow breaths seemed to catch in my chest. We all knew they were telling me something I should already have known about people who belonged to me. I said I had to go to the bathroom. I allowed for a moment in which Margaret could say she'd come with me, but she didn't. She remained where she was with her arms crossed, standing between Bea and Olivia. If she came with me, we'd probably never find them again. But if I left Margaret, I might not be able to find her either, which meant she'd decided. Whatever happened to me next that night didn't necessarily have to involve her.

I walked fast through the blare of the fairgrounds. I felt dazed. I felt like the music of my life had suddenly cut off, leaving me alone on the dance floor, sweating and disoriented in the musicless air. Shame's mighty drumbeat swelled to fill the vacuum, pounding in time with my heart. I skimmed the faces in the crowd as I walked. There were so many versions of myself running around this weird party, so many brown-haired white girls in deliberately small clothing holding their phones, holding their friends' hands, taking each other's pictures, eating each other's food, embarrassing themselves and realizing it, realizing they were tired and pretending they didn't want to go home, girls who were drunk, girls who were crying, girls who were tying each other's shoes and fixing each other's hair, girls with eyeliner smudged by sweat, girls radiant in the artificial light. I could have been any of them. There was no reason in the world I had to be myself except that I was.

Fairgoers gave up on the regiment of portable bathrooms at night. Boys relieved themselves in the grass beside the reeking blue chambers. They pissed at the fair's perimeter. I passed rows of boys with straightened posture, their hands down their pants as though guiding a rudder, their chins a little upright. The girls made more of an effort to disguise themselves, walking in pairs toward the opaque woods that abutted the fairgrounds. I fell in among them and soon left behind the fair's broad lights.

I tried to stray from the most obviously trodden paths and found the unused parts of the woods dense with brush. Great bushes tangled at the feet of trees and between them grew dense weeds and grasses, a mass of blackened foliage. When I turned on my phone's flashlight, bugs swarmed to meet the beam, a cone fluorescing in the dark.

"We can watch for you," a voice said from behind me. "We already went."

I turned around to see two girls standing surprisingly close to me. The one speaking had a round face and heavy winged eyeliner. The other had a hand on her hip and an engraved metal flask in the other. They both appeared at ease, as though it were the most natural thing in the world that they should be drunk and helping a stranger pee in the woods, whereas for me, this was an event. I was entering for the first time in my life a real link into the chain of great bathroom encounters between girls who don't know each other.

"No one is coming," the girl with the flask said. "But we'll watch in case."

I thanked them shyly, turned off my flashlight, and slid my phone into my shorts pocket. I walked a few more paces into the trees, too afraid of the night to go farther but not wanting to pee directly next to people I'd just met. I had to stomp on a patch of waist-high grass and then slide my foot across the ground to hold it down and create a space for myself to squat. The girls stood sentinel mere feet behind me, our backs to each other. Blades of grass began to come undone, scratching against my legs and bare ass. I hesitated. I cursed having a body. But then the girls began to talk to each other, in an easy, general way, and their voices gave me cover. I let myself begin and willed myself to hurry.

Then I was up and quickly returning. The woods righted themselves behind me, erasing where I'd stood. The first girl handed me hand sanitizer from her purse. We all turned to leave. I reached for my pockets and audibly inhaled.

"My phone," I said.

My phone had slid from the too-small container of my shorts into the opaque brush beneath me. I'd never get back to Margaret. I'd never find a ride home. The only number I had memorized was my mother's, which meant I'd have to call her. I'd have to call my mom on some stranger's phone and tell her I'd lost my phone and my friends and ask if she'd drive all the way out here and pick me up. I'd have to wait a long time for her to drive down the highway to fetch me, the stupidest girl in the world. My throat tightened. I was ready to cry.

"Don't worry, bb," the girl with the flask said. Her eyes were glazed, but her voice was clear. "We'll find it. You just had it. It's here."

Endearments from people I didn't know usually made me itch, but the confidence in her voice, the way the two of them began moving in calm and systematic steps, up and down, bent half over with their phones held out in front of them, flashlights on, eyes trained to the ground when they could have just left, made me flush with gratitude that I wasn't alone.

"Found it," the eyelinered girl said, her voice deep and raspy. She held my phone up in the air for me to see. Her short fingernails were painted shiny black. Relief popped like confetti in my brain. I hugged them.

"Oh my God," I said. "Thank you!" And then, "Are you my fairy godmothers?"

They looked at each other and laughed. The look held an intimacy, a mutual ownership I thought I recognized. There was more than one reason two girls might leave the fair for the privacy of the woods. This possibility emboldened me. Besides, I loved to trust someone. I was tired of having no one to trust, and also I felt in that moment that the world had delivered me into their presence, and that the world knew better than I did, that it had to, because I knew nothing, and in that case, it was alright to ask.

"I have a question for you, if that's okay," I said. They nodded. "My best friend kissed me," I went on. "And not in the regular way. In a different, on-the-mouth way. But she won't talk to me about it or acknowledge that it happened, which could have meant she thought the kiss was casual. But then, she gave me a printed picture of herself naked, which was not casual. Like, she fully gave me a picture of herself naked to look at. But she still acts like I've never seen her naked except in the normal ways I've seen her naked."

"Lol the normal ways," said the girl with the black eyeliner and fingernails. "What are the normal ways?" Her voice held an almost sarcastic lilt, but I could tell she took what I'd said seriously, as though this were a question she had previously asked herself.

"The ways that aren't on purpose," I said, though I knew it didn't exactly make sense.

She closed her eyes and then opened them, looking me dead on. "Anytime you choose to be naked with someone, you choose to be naked with someone."

I nodded. "The girl I mean," I said. "She was here with me today, and then she left me and my other friend here alone and went home. What should I do?"

The girl with the flask swayed a little. Then she rested her chin on her friend's shoulder and considered. "Okay, the highest-key thing you could do is send a picture like right now. Not a picture you've already taken, a picture you take right now, when she knows you're out here without her, but she doesn't know exactly what you're doing. Then she'll be like, fuck, what am I missing?"

"Great idea," her friend said. "Incredible idea." She tilted her face against her friend's, still resting on her shoulder. "She used to do that to me, and it made me feel deranged."

I wanted El to feel deranged. I wanted to derange Eleanor.

"You could take off your shirt," she said. "To make it even with what she gave you."

"No, I can't," I answered, suddenly nervous that once again I wasn't up to the task of being a teenager.

"That's fine," she reassured me. "You look fly already."

I nodded, moved by her gentleness, and took a step back. The eyelinered girl squatted down to the ground with my phone. The other put her flask in her little purple purse and held her flashlight up to illuminate me.

"Now walk toward us," she said.

So I walked toward them with what I hoped to be an alluring expression on my face, my cheeks slightly drawn between my teeth for the sake of my cheekbones, and she tapped the round white button many times, and then we all huddled around my phone to review the results. Our foreheads touched. My illuminated silhouette cut against the massive vertical lines made by the trees around me. I looked intriguing. I looked like a gesture toward my most beautiful self while in the middle of doing something unexplained. It was the kind of picture Eleanor would appreciate. I didn't let myself agonize over which of the minutely different images was best. I chose one and sent it to her immediately.

The girls walked me back out of the woods maybe twenty minutes after I'd entered it. I wanted to hold both their hands but felt shy. We followed each other online before we parted. Margaret of course wasn't where I'd left her, and her phone went straight to voicemail. I wondered if she'd even noticed yet that it had died. If I'd lost someone, I would have waited for them at our last meeting place. Instead, Margaret had wandered off. It would take her forever to come looking for me, even though her mom was due to pick us up in half an hour. She'd use the whole thing as an excuse to be late to the carpool line. I had to find her.

As I stared at the space where Margaret should have been standing, worry flashed through me, quickly replaced by indignation. We shouldn't have been separated in the first place. She should have come with me to the woods in order to explain what had happened with Eleanor. She should have been the one to take my picture and tell me how good I looked. In a group of two people, these were the rules of the bathroom: You didn't go alone.

BY THE TIME I FOUND MARGARET, SHE LOOKED DIFFERENT. SHE was standing in line for the freshly squeezed lemonade the fair sold in souvenir cups, and she'd put her sweat-curled hair up into a ponytail on top of her head, the tips blond. Bea and Olivia were gone. Instead, she lingered among a knot of people I didn't know, telling a story in over-the-top terms. She tipped her head back to laugh deliberately. She always provided just a little bit more than was called for in a given situation, and people found this a relief. In her presence, they could do less. They could participate in her momentum. But she was so good at offering this to people that sometimes they partook in her as an experience instead of treating her as a person. Which pissed me off. I didn't like when people did that to her, and I didn't like when she let them.

Her conspiratorial tone of voice, her exaltation of the inappropriate, the taboo, the more—these facets of her personality, which I loved, also served to entertain other people, which I hated. First because I wasn't sure she understood the difference between what I gave her in my friendship and what everyone else did, as though my love were fungible for the love of other people. And second because she really did need the love of people who weren't me or even other people specifically, like Eleanor. She needed the opportunity to react to the presence of generalized, even anonymous, social attention, which made me afraid.

Margaret made me afraid that I lacked some connection with the world, a connection she knew how to access that I did not.

"TG you found me," she said, the abbreviation deliberately casual and offhand, cutting off my complaints before I could make them. "You were gone for eighty years." She didn't withdraw from the lemonade line or the group she'd been talking to, so I had to answer to everyone and at least attempt to match her tone.

"I lost my phone in the woods and found it again. Classic."

"Mine is dead," she said. "Can you text my mom we're fine?"

Nancy answered almost immediately. She wanted my confirmation that we were ready to leave. Margaret took the phone from me to type out a brief and noncommittal affirmative. She wanted to leave room for any last-minute possibilities. Nancy responded again, wanting us to reiterate the location where we'd agreed to meet. This was a game they'd taught each other how to play.

"I don't know what we're doing next," Margaret said to the group when asked by one of them.

I gave her a look that meant we needed time to get to the parking lot on the other side of the fair, and she gave me a look that meant once her mom arrived, she wouldn't leave without us, and therefore punctuality was unimportant. Nancy had to wait if we made her. My phone vibrated again.

"She's here," I said. That's how long I'd had to wander around before I found Margaret.

"She's saying that because she wants us to start walking."

Even if that were true, Margaret was bargaining with me over mere minutes. I imagined Nancy, having driven almost an hour to retrieve us, arriving at the front of the car line to find that we weren't there. People holding neon-orange batons would try to tell her she had to go to the back of the line and circle around. She'd roll down the window and yell for sure.

My phone started ringing.

"Fine, let me say goodbye," Margaret said.

She hugged each individual person and told them how pretty they were and insisted they all go to the theater to see the horror movie I'd refused to attend because I didn't need any additional reasons to be afraid or have my heart beat fast. When Nancy called again, I held out the phone.

"Pick up and tell her we're by the exit but don't see her yet."

If Margaret said so, her mom wouldn't believe her, but if I said so, she would. Margaret wanted to make use of my credibility.

"I'm not going to do that," I said.

She looked at me like I was the one who owed her a favor, like offering to let me lie to her mom was an act of generosity on her part that I had been too stupid to accept.

"Okay, then tell her we were confused and went to the other exit but are on our way to her now, since we are."

I also wasn't doing that. I simply wasn't going to pick up my phone and lie to Margaret's mother for the sake of fixing a problem she'd knowingly created, one I'd tried to prevent.

"Let's just go," I said, and put my phone into my backpack. If we didn't pick up, then we wouldn't have anything to explain. I thought Margaret would protest further, but instead she nodded. She'd already established me as the friend who'd refused to help when asked, which I realized had been part of the point of her asking. She wanted me in the wrong.

We took off toward the exit. I ran faster than Margaret and surged ahead of her, weaving through the crowd, spurred on by anger and the strange pleasure of running through a crowd at night. Ten minutes later I got to the exit, breathless and spiked by adrenaline. I saw a massive shining pickup truck, a black station wagon, three silver vehicles all in a row. None of them was Margaret's mom's car. When Margaret appeared a minute later beside me, she laughed.

She paused to catch her breath, resting her hands on her knees. Then she stood up and deliberately didn't look at me, mad that I'd once again made things difficult when they didn't have to be, that I'd ended her night early unnecessarily. The candied lights of the fair loomed behind us. Only narrow white beams from the waiting cars split the darkness of the parking lot. Margaret began to scan the groups milling around us, looking for anyone she knew or recognized, checking to see if there was a person on earth she could talk to other than me. God forbid a single minute should pass without some sort of stimulation to entertain her.

"You can't tell me to lie to your mom," I snapped. "You know I can't do that. It's honestly mean of you to ask me to do that."

Instead of responding, Margaret checked the line of cars again. She saw no reason to argue with me or even acknowledge what I'd said. The night would be over soon enough. She pushed her bracelets up and down her wrists. The scene in the lot was almost quiet, the high buzz of the fair behind us, each call from a car audible and distinct.

When I opened my mouth to speak again, Margaret glared and cut me off. "Actually," she said under her breath, "it's a very normal thing for a person to do for their supposedly best friend." My chest constricted. "I'm not asking you to hide a crisis," she went on. "Like you literally cannot bring yourself to imply we're in one parking lot when we're supposed to be in another?"

Her voice was terse, irritable, haughty. Margaret hated fighting with anyone other than her mother, and I knew she especially hated that I was forcing us to have a confrontation in public. I crossed my arms.

"That's exactly my point," I said. "You want me to lie for your convenience, just so you can have fifteen additional seconds of mediocre fun. No, not even fun, just the appearance of fun, the slim possibility of fun, just to be absolutely sure there isn't any fun being had by anyone in the world that you're not a part of."

"What am I asking that is so unreasonable?" she shot back. "You're the one who turns every regular situation into a problem, based on a moral code you don't even follow."

An SUV at the front was holding up the line. Some friend of the passengers leaned through their open window, saying a protracted goodbye. The cars behind them began to honk and flash their lights.

In the commotion, I raised my voice. "I'm sorry, what?"

"You didn't really lose your phone in the woods."

What a bizarre allegation.

"I did lose my phone in the woods."

"You kissed Eleanor!" Margaret cried accusingly, as though I'd torn the words from her. The car beside us laid on its horn. She lowered her voice to say, "I know because *she* told me—immediately, right after it happened."

And I hadn't. I felt an immense downward pressure, like gravity had accelerated for me personally. My neck bent into my shoulders defensively. The SUV at last pulled out of its spot at the front, and the line of cars behind it reanimated. White beams from the moving vehicles flared across my sight.

"You knew?" I whisper-screamed. "You knew—and you kissed her!" The revelation of Margaret's betrayal crowded out my awareness of my own. I allowed it to. "What is wrong with you?" I'd hardly ever kissed anyone in my life. Before Eleanor, I'd never kissed a girl. I'd certainly never kissed anyone I loved, and I'd loved Eleanor before she kissed me, even if it was a love I hadn't been aware could yield that kind of desire. The tangled immensity of my feelings for Eleanor, all my thwarted efforts to return us to that brief and perfect moment of transparency on the field, the way she'd left me, again, only a few hours ago after so nearly saying aloud at last what she wanted—all of it rose up in a great tide within me, and the first tears trembled in my eyes. I willed them not to fall.

"We all kiss each other all the time," Margaret said, pushing back. "Who cares?" But she wouldn't look at me, refusing to observe my obvious feeling. The stakes of kissing Eleanor, our best friend, were different than the stakes of kissing anyone else, and intuitively, she knew that. Just like I knew that kissing someone in a game, in front of and for an audience, wasn't the same as kissing them when you were alone, though I didn't say so. I needed Margaret to acknowledge the betrayal before I could concede to its mitigating circumstances.

"You're not allowed to kiss Eleanor anymore," I said quietly, my voice like a stretched rubber band in my throat that I couldn't allow to snap. I did not want to cry in this parking lot.

Margaret scoffed. "Because all of the sudden you like her?"

"Not all of the sudden." It had been weeks. It had been the whole summer spent wishing. It had been before that too, though I hadn't realized.

Margaret raised her chin. "And how was I supposed to know that?" A fair and unfair question. She was the daughter of a lawyer. I was the one who'd failed to tell her Eleanor kissed me. I was the one who hadn't been honest about how I felt. But I recognized the look on her face as the one she gave her mother when she knew she'd done something wrong but could still win the argument. It was a look that had, more than once, led her mom to break a plate.

"You did know," I said, realizing this was true, my voice creaking, tears falling hot and fast on my cheeks now. "You knew."

She shook her head, but her eyes remained on the cars, her arms crossed, determined.

I'd never had to tell Margaret how I felt in order for her to read my feelings. I shouldn't have had to ask Margaret not to hurt me, even in ways I hadn't explicitly said I could be hurt. Not when she knew. Not when I'd never made her notarize her own vulnerabilities—the ones that were too painful for her to say aloud—before I started trying to protect her from them. She'd known, and still she'd done this to me. For my silence, maybe she'd chosen to punish me.

"You don't get to tell me how to be a good friend," she said.

A sob clawed its way out of my chest and broke into my mouth. I did my best to smother the sound. I wiped my nose with the back of my hand. Margaret's face turned red. She seemed to inch farther away from me, her eyes darting over my shoulder. The other kids in the parking lot gave us plenty of space. No one stood in our immediate vicinity, though they must have been watching or at least aware, while they lingered waiting for their rides. I was too overwhelmed to turn around and check whether or not we'd gained an audience. I almost didn't care. None of these people mattered to me. Teenage girls always manage to have their hearts broken at least once in a public place.

"Why didn't you just tell me, once you knew?" I asked when I'd caught my breath.

At last, Margaret looked at me. Tears had appeared in her eyes, but she blinked them back. "Why didn't you just tell me you kissed her?" she asked.

In reply, I wanted to scream and then vomit on my shoes. I couldn't answer. I didn't all the way know why myself. I hadn't truly considered the decision as I made and sustained it, as the weeks passed, weeks in which Margaret's coldness had held me at a distance, a distance for which I now saw I was responsible.

I knew everyone Margaret had ever kissed. She'd told me right away, as they happened. I knew what the boys had been wearing, what their underwear looked like. I even knew the size of their dicks as measured by her hand. But none of those boys had been Eleanor. None of them had been our best friend.

The parade of vehicles began to move more swiftly, pairs of lights pulling past us, briefly spotlighting our faces. When Nancy's car slid up in front of us, Margaret climbed into the front seat. I sat in the back. Margaret didn't bother to accuse her mother of having lied about the time of her arrival. She didn't complain about the fact that we'd been waiting for her to show up. Neither of us said anything at all, which made Nancy look at Margaret and then at me through the rearview mirror, trying to understand what had happened between us.

I watched the highway while Nancy drove, the dashed line of glowing streetlamps, the orange taillights before us, and the white high beams heading in our direction. I kept my eyes on these bright stamps against the black surface of night as they blurred and rippled before me, never glancing into the passenger-side mirror, because I didn't want to see Margaret's righteous anger, her conviction of having been wronged by me or, beneath it, her sadness.

I asked to be taken to my house instead of Margaret's. When Nancy pulled into my driveway, I got out of the car, and Nancy lingered until she saw me open the front door. She seemed to want to give me a chance to change my mind. I waved to indicate my thanks. Margaret would know the wave was meant for her mother.

I had to run to disable and then reset the house alarm, then up the stairs to reassure my parents I wasn't an intruder, merely their daughter arriving home instead of spending the night where she'd said she'd be. I whispered I was going to bed.

My dad mumbled, "Alright."

I thought for a moment that my mom, who always knew everything, would wake up and demand I tell her what was wrong. I waited in case she did, but she only rolled over in her sleep. I closed the door and walked to the bathroom, where I took off all my clothes but didn't wash my face or brush my teeth. Nor did I turn on any lights, just felt my way around in the dark. Then I got into bed naked, put my softest pillow on top of my face, and wondered what was wrong with me.

I remembered a conversation I'd had with Margaret the previous summer. Her mom had dropped us off at the mall. We went to the makeup store to play with deeply used eyeshadow samples, and Margaret told me her dad was moving out.

"His new apartment is so clean," she said, and pressed a line of metallic-blue powder across her inner wrist. "I didn't know he cared about cleanliness."

Margaret's house, as long as I'd known it, was densely populated with objects: mail, receipts, potted plants, and spilled purses. It's terrible to discover that what you had considered a family trait in fact belongs to only one parent and is perhaps barely tolerated by the other.

"That's disturbing," I said. I walked to the end of the aisle to soak a cotton swab in makeup remover. The back of my hand was striped with shades of lip gloss I wanted to clear away. When I returned, I found Margaret in front of a floating circular mirror, using an index finger to hold down one of her eyelids.

"Oh my God, don't," I said. "Don't actually put that on your eyes, please."

She stuck out her tongue at me. She held up the middle finger of her other hand and then used it to swipe purple pigment across her eyelid.

"Ugh, looks terrible," she said, examining the results in the mirror.

"Close your eyes," I replied. She closed them, and her eyelids quivered. "Don't actually close them all the way," I amended. "Just look down."

She looked down, and her eyelid stayed flat. With my makeup-remover swab, I carefully retraced the line Margaret had made to remove the purple without disturbing the rest of her makeup, but I had to hold the swab steady by balancing the heel of my hand against the top of her cheek. When I pulled my hand away, a thin coat of her tinted foundation remained on my skin. She blinked several times and examined herself in the mirror.

"I'm sorry this is happening. When does he officially move out?" I asked. It occurred to me that if my dad moved into an apartment by himself, I had no idea what the apartment would look like.

"A month ago," she answered, and walked off toward the perfume aisle.

The things Margaret didn't tell me obeyed a limit of significance. Minor pleasures and embarrassments she might keep to herself, but if something really important happened, she'd tell me. If not at once, then soon. If not soon, then eventually. I had only to tolerate the interim. This was the condition on which

I allowed Margaret to keep the secrets she did without feeling wounded.

Once I know what a rule is, the rule becomes reason and weapon enough to corral my feelings. Margaret knew that about me. She understood the threshold of nondisclosure I would accept, and she required no promise of threshold from me in return because I'd never kept anything from her in the first place, not before Eleanor.

I didn't run after Margaret and ask why she hadn't told me as soon as her dad mentioned leaving or signed a lease or packed his bags or actually left. I knew why. She didn't want it to be true. She wanted our friendship to exist for as long as possible as though her father still lived in her house.

I would have blown up our friendship, the dynamic between the three of us, by kissing Eleanor more if she'd let me, but she didn't let me. Instead, she became suddenly close with Margaret in a way I suddenly wasn't—the result, I now knew, of her honesty and my lack thereof—such that I became preoccupied instead with trying to return us to how we'd been. I wanted Margaret to go back to being my best friend. I wanted to reassume our old standard of closeness. That was my priority. Only then could I consider trusting her with my secrets and desires. A flawed configuration of events, it was now clear to me, for secrets and desires are at the heart of our selfhood, and no one can be your best friend if you don't let them see who you are.

The pillow on top of my face created a comforting double dark. Soon I closed my eyes and slept heavily until morning.

I SPENT THE NEXT FEW DAYS FEELING HORRIBLE. I MASTURBATED sadly and took naps. At night, I stayed up, staring out my window at the moon and thinking grandiose thoughts about my loneliness.

Margaret had never really been mad at me before. I'd been mad at her, and she'd been irritable with me. She'd canceled our plans and taken too long to text me back and hung out with other people, but her resistance to outright conflict meant she'd never quite accused me of doing anything wrong. She'd certainly never accused me of an outright breach of our friendship. The presence of her name in my phone moved gradually lower in the queue of my text messages, neither of us saying anything. A hard pebble of dread knocked around in my stomach.

Eleanor didn't say much either. She appeared to be experiencing a vulnerability hangover from having communicated so much to me at the fair and, as was her by-then established habit, she withdrew. She claimed in the group chat to be very busy with tennis practice. Was the purpose of this message to remind me that somewhere within a five-mile radius of my house she was then wearing pastel-colored miniskirts and shouting violently whenever she stroked a forehand into the corner? Regardless of intent, the message had this effect.

As a result, I was at home on Thursday morning and available to be tricked by my mother into running an errand with her.

I'd already agreed to escort her to the bakery to buy sandwiches for lunch because if I asked her to bring me back a cookie, she'd remind me that a person should only have one dessert a day and decline, but if I went to the bakery with her, then I could order the cookie at the counter myself. My mom respected driving anywhere as a reason to buy dessert. So, she had me in the car.

"Why are we here?" I asked in the parking lot of the pharmacy we'd just turned in to unannounced.

She said my dad had a prescription that needed picking up. I couldn't stay in the car, because its seats were black, the lot had no shade, and the sun beat down with relentless enthusiasm. When the automatic glass doors of the store parted, its refrigerated air breathed onto my neck and made me shiver. I wanted to get home as soon as possible. Out in public, I felt exposed. I could run into Margaret or Eleanor or their mothers or one of my mother's acquaintances or anyone at any minute, and I felt a vehement fear of being perceived or having to account for myself.

"Why are we doing this now, though?" I asked. "You could have come back later." Later, when I wasn't in the middle of an ongoing crisis, whenever and if ever that would be.

"Would you have preferred to leave the house twice?" my mom asked while she shook a red plastic shopping basket loose from its stack.

"No, you could have come back by yourself," I said.

I knew this was a mean, fundamentally illogical, petulant, childish thing to say and that I'd definitely say more similar things if I didn't remove myself from my mother's presence that minute, so I stalked into the hair-care aisle and began examining labels. *Pharmacies are ugly,* I purposefully thought to myself about the white metal aisles and fluorescent lighting. In fact, I loved pharmacies and their bizarre assortment of offerings, like the seasonal aisle, which at that time of year contained both water guns and purses, but I couldn't risk any resulting amelioration of mood.

Once I stopped being angry, I'd have to start being sad. I wanted to feel only that my friends were terrible, careless people. I knew that they loved me. People who love you do not, however, exclusively behave in your best interest. Still, in the whole time we'd been friends, none of us had ever acted with the express purpose of hurting each other. My throat felt dry with misery.

My mother perused the aisles at a full meander. I'd never seen the woman in a hurry in my life. Her height meant I could watch her brown-and-silver head of hair on its slow journey from the first-aid section to the aisle with tissues and toilet paper.

I told myself that maybe if Eleanor had kissed me twice, I would have told Margaret. That if she'd texted me back or taken off her shirt in my presence instead of in a picture she didn't even tell me she'd given, I would have said something. If she'd made whatever existed between us real by acknowledging its reality. But then I remembered that in fact she had acknowledged its reality, because she'd told Margaret. She just didn't tell me she'd done so. Because she was Eleanor, I hadn't thought she'd want to tell anyone. Since she'd acted like kissing me was a secret, I thought it was supposed to be. But Margaret was her best friend, and you tell your best friend when you kiss someone. You tell your best friend everything, including other people's secrets.

Once Eleanor told Margaret, Margaret should have told me she knew, but I should have already told Margaret about Eleanor in the first place, even if Eleanor hadn't wanted me to, for the same reason Eleanor had told Margaret: Margaret was my best friend, and I always told her everything. For the first time, I hadn't wanted to, which was why I didn't, in the parking lot, immediately apologize to Margaret. A stubborn voice within me said I hadn't been wrong to keep the secret, though when I asked this voice further questions about my behavior, it had very little to say.

When my mom finally got into line for the prescription counter, I joined her. If she asked the pharmacist a question when she got to the front, I thought I might expire.

"It's freezing in here," I said. She responded by sending me back to find her preferred brand of probiotics. "Why do you forget something every time we enter a line?" I asked.

"Because I'm managing the day-to-day existence and mental and emotional well-being of three people simultaneously," she responded, then answered her phone on its first ring.

She said things like this to me repeatedly, but I couldn't understand them then. I couldn't understand the nature of her life's work or the incredible feat of its intelligence, the keeping of all of us alive enough to pursue our personal plotlines, or what that keeping entailed. I recognized many aspects of the project of living as arbitrary and so made the mistake of considering them optional. All the time with my mother I wondered, *Do we really have to be doing this?*

My phone vibrated with a message from Eleanor, the first since her note about tennis. I deposited the probiotics into my mom's basket and signaled I'd meet her by the car. Whatever El sent me, I wanted to look at it by myself. Outside, midday heat cooked the parking lot blacktop. There were plenty of open spaces. I leaned my hip against the car door and then jerked backward, the olive-green metal blazing against my bare thigh. I had to use my hand to shade the screen of my phone while I opened her message.

I'd sent Eleanor my picture from the fair via DM instead of text as an offer to ignore that she'd been ignoring me. Eleanor didn't like explaining herself, and she didn't really know how to do it. Among the three of us, for the most part, Margaret told stories, I explained them, and Eleanor asked provocative questions. Sending her the picture this way also meant I knew when she opened it. *Seen Saturday* had read the little gray text beneath my message. Saturday was the night of the fair. Had Eleanor spent the days since determining how to reply?

She'd liked my picture—a heart appeared in its lower left corner—and she'd sent back a screenshot of a Sim swooning. I liked the screenshot. Now what? What was I supposed to do? How do you turn a person into your girlfriend when you're currently mad at them and ultimately unclear on their feelings for you? I didn't have anyone to ask, so I spent the drive to the bakery reading the internet, which had plenty of advice on the general topic of best friends to lovers but could not instruct me specifically on how to exist in relation to Eleanor or tell me whose turn it was to do what. What are the steps of loving? They exist uniquely between every two people who attempt to climb them.

THE COMPLETE AND UNPRECEDENTED HALT OF ALL CONTACT WITH Margaret changed my dynamic with Eleanor because Eleanor had been using Margaret and our shared forums of communication as a backdoor means of talking to me without actually having to talk to me. Margaret, I realized, had known this, tolerated such a role all summer, and finally grown sick of it. She canceled coming to Eleanor's parents' anniversary party by telling Eleanor only, forcing Eleanor to choose—reach out to me directly for the first time in nearly two months or allow me to show up at her house, find out Margaret wasn't there, and plausibly interpret her lack of advance notice as a desire to be alone with me.

I realized this when Eleanor texted me at the last minute, the morning of the party, on the first Saturday of August. On her phone, I knew, would have been her single blue message on the right side of the screen facing a wall of gray text on the left from me, all the messages I'd sent and then deleted from my message history. I didn't even remember what I'd said exactly, which was both horrible and a gift. I noted that Eleanor had chosen not to message me in the separate DM thread I'd opened by sending her my picture. I wondered if she wondered if I'd cancel. I wondered if she knew about what happened between me and Margaret. I didn't know what terms the two of them were on with each other by now. I texted back a sad-face emoji in response to the news of Margaret's absence. If Eleanor didn't want to be alone with me, she'd have to tell me not to come.

Later, I ran up the stairs to my mother's bedroom. All her windows were open. Still in her cotton nightgown, she was typing on her laptop, pieces of paper scattered across the rest of the bed. A lawnmower buzzed at intervals of increasing and then decreasing volume as it moved back and forth across a lawn somewhere down the street.

"Are you going to tell me you need to tell Eleanor's mom that we kissed before I'm allowed to sleep over at her house by myself?" I asked. I'd rather never have a sleepover again for the rest of my life than be the one responsible for Kim finding out that we kissed.

"It's a problem," my mom said, shifting the computer from her lap. She talked and moved so slowly. "I'm not going to tell Eleanor's mom," she eventually announced, "because it isn't my business. But I need to ask you, do you want to sleep there? Not only because you've already said yes?"

"Yeah," I said.

She pushed herself into a more upright seated position. "And you know that I would come and get you for any reason?"

"Yes." The question was under what circumstances I'd be willing to call her.

"And if you want to, you can still change your mind and say that you're not allowed to have sleepovers yet?"

"Okay, I know."

Some bird on the tree nearest to the bedroom windows began to warble, then cry.

"You have to be responsible for your own good judgment," my mom said, "but I do wish Kim had somewhat less confidence that everything always turns out for the best."

I gave her a little hug and ran away.

OSCILLATING WATER SPRINKLERS WAVED LIKE enormous hands across the green expanse of Eleanor's lawn. My mom walked me up to the front of the house. Moms always want to enter and exit through the official egress of a building. Kim opened the door to greet us with her white blown-dry hair and bearing of official welcome. Eleanor stood behind her mother. I stood behind mine.

While they went through their salutations, Eleanor and I examined each other. She wore her hair in a high, tight ponytail, the bones of her face elfin, the rosacea on her cheeks pink, her feet bare. She watched my eyes dip to the metal script of her necklace and then return to her face. It was as much of an admission as I was able to make.

Yes, I was mad at Eleanor. I could have called her to account, but more than why she told Margaret about kissing me, I wanted to know what she said and how she said it. I wished I could have seen her face when she used my name in a sentence about herself. We didn't have to break eye contact, because we weren't alone, though it still took some courage to keep my gaze steady.

"Thank you for lending us Mina," Kim said. Part of her charm lay in giving other people the opportunity to feel gracious.

"Oh, you're welcome," my mom answered, smiling but unable to leap into friendly banter without additional social runway.

My parents and Margaret's mother had all been invited to this party but declined. My mom declined all invitations to parties at which she wouldn't know a significant portion of the guest list, and Margaret's mom said no because she hadn't yet gotten used to attending events without a husband.

"Ellie enjoys occasions like this so much more with a friend," Kim said. She talked with her hands, heavy gold and silver bracelets jumping up and down her wrists when she gestured. I winced before I could remember not to.

"Yes, thank you for *lending* us Mina," Eleanor said, her tone the vocal equivalent of an eye roll. She hated this form of her mother's courtesy—the implication of a deficiency within the self for the sake of thanking someone else for filling it in. She didn't want to congratulate anyone for help she didn't need. She didn't want to need anything from anybody at all.

As soon as the sentence had left her mouth, she felt embarrassed. I saw it on her face. Her sarcasm had been too sharp, too private, meant either for her mother or for me but not for the two of us together at the same time, and certainly not for my mother.

"Mina does that to me too," my mom reassured Eleanor. What she lacked in ease, she made up for in alertness to the emotional environment and a resulting compassionate sincerity.

"Oh, teenagers are ruthless," Kim replied, having raised five of them. "Ellie's sisters used to steal my reading glasses and then wear them to tell me my behavior disappointed them terribly."

She invited my mom in for a glass of iced tea in spite of the approaching deadline of the party. She'd thrown too many of them to feel anxious. Instead, she appeared energized by the prospect of the evening. My mom politely declined entering the house, but before she left she had one last thing to say, and she gave me a quick look before she began speaking—a moment to prepare myself for embarrassment.

"The girls are sleeping here tonight," she confirmed. "If there's any change of plans, please call."

"Of course," Kim said with a smile. "No camping or decamping." But when she saw that my mom couldn't treat the events of that June with humor, she went on, "You have my number if there's anything you need."

Despite the ten-year age gap between them and the differences in approach with respect to me and Eleanor, I always thought our moms could have been friends. Each in their own way, they took themselves and their daughters very seriously. But Kim had already made friends with the mothers of her older children's classmates, and my mom never initiated a new relationship without quite a lot of encouragement from the other side.

She left. We all waved to her from the front door. Then Kim turned to me and Eleanor.

"Ladies, we have three hours," she said.

THE PRETENSE OF THE PARTY freed me and Eleanor from having to make sense of each other right away. Kim required our best and most helpful attitudes. We ran up and down the slick wooden hallways of the first floor, giggling and sliding in our socks between the errands Kim assigned us, fetching drink dispensers from the basement, chopping up fruit for fruit salad, slicing cheese for cheese plates, and hurrying outside to arrange napkins and placemats on the long line of tables set up in the backyard and stab teak torches into the ground at even intervals in a rectangular perimeter to keep mosquitoes at bay.

The secret I'd thought I had with Eleanor turned out to be a secret Eleanor had with Margaret. This gave me a kind of power. Having been wounded awards you the right to a concessionary gesture. But acting wounded or requesting concession would have ruined all our running around and laughing, so I didn't. We scoured the garden with kitchen shears, cutting flowers for bouquets. When I leaned over some waist-high foliage to reach the thin neck of a poppy, my hair slid over my shoulder onto the leaves. Eleanor, quick and decisive, flashed out her scissors to snip the end from a curl. The crisp sound of the metal slicing through my hair made me gasp. My lock fell into the garden. I gave her a look.

"I live here now," I said, and cut another flower.

When the catering staff arrived, we traipsed upstairs to get ready. The audible stacking of plates, jingling of silverware, voices, and footsteps that rose from the first floor and backyard of the house through her bedroom's open windows helped soften the sensation of our being alone together.

"What are you wearing?" I asked.

If she were Margaret, I would have already known. Discarded shirts, skirts, and tank tops lay on the floor, evidence of a decision-making process. She held up a short black shift dress with puffed sleeves, a silky black bow for her ponytail. I half-laughed when I pulled out my own clothing, a linen dress of the same length in white and a white headband. We'd match, or rather we'd offset each other precisely. It was like I almost knew what she wanted from me.

Kim knocked on the door and then stuck her head around to check on our progress. Her eyes immediately moved to the rumpled clothes on the carpet.

"No one is coming in here," Eleanor said defensively. "No one is allowed to be in here."

"I remember," Kim answered, "but shut the windows. Some people will want to come inside for a break from the heat."

Guests began to arrive, but we remained in Eleanor's room. She hated having to greet people one at a time, so we sat on her floor fully dressed and waited. Her phone illuminated with a text from Margaret. We both saw Margaret's name appear on her screen. She turned her phone over.

"Are you mad at Mar?" I asked.

"No," Eleanor replied. "That's a stupid question." And then, "A little bit." She started absentmindedly folding one of the shirts, which I now realized she'd left out to deter her mother from including her room in tours of the house. Then she caught herself and threw the shirt back on the floor. "My mom buys me things just so she can show them to other people," she said.

The party had risen to life beneath us. We could hear the chatter of people and clinking of glasses, cars approaching, and music moving through the house.

"Let's go downstairs," she said.

ELEANOR'S OLDER BROTHERS AND SISTERS had all been charming party participants throughout their shared childhood and adolescence. Eleanor resented the assumption that she would or could do the same. Her siblings, after all, had had each other, whereas Eleanor had to diffuse the attention of so many adults on her own, adults who were inevitably too charmed by the presence of a blond daughter. Eleanor once told me she wanted to dye her hair. I tried not to look horrified, because mothers, not friends, are the ones who look horrified when you suggest changing yourself.

"Your mom and I have known each other for a lifetime, it feels like," a woman said to Eleanor, carrying a glass of white wine, in which floated pieces of frozen fruit.

"Isn't she remarkably popular?" Eleanor said.

Eleanor was suspicious of popularity. She knew that when people liked you too much, they wanted something in return.

"Oh yes," the woman agreed, and her husband appeared beside her.

"Ellie," he said, and I felt her stiffen. "How tall you've grown since the last time we saw you." He put a congenial hand on her shoulder that I wanted to remove.

"Yes," she said. "The last time you saw me was at my sister's wedding. I was twelve."

"Exactly," he agreed with good humor, pleased to have apparently been remembered. "That's right."

Adults rarely noticed when Eleanor was in the middle of calling them idiots. This had to do with her tone of voice, so deliciously deadpan it resembled the version of sincerity most people attribute to teenage girls. On top of that, her hair, her young attractive femaleness, the approaching precipice of her mature appearance, her parents, her siblings, and her own more accommodating behavior at a younger age—which she now considered traitorous—all conspired to create a seemingly impenetrable barrier to her real personality. Adults didn't believe in her bad moods or her sarcasm. All her weapons, which I so admired, hardly produced the effect their sharp points deserved. This insensibility disappointed Eleanor, though it likewise permitted her to wield those weapons more brazenly.

I put my right arm around her shoulder, and she put her left arm around my waist, and when the next person to stop us made as though to hug Eleanor in greeting, neither of us moved, and they were forced to shift their weight to retract the gesture. I gave a blank smile as I introduced myself, which Eleanor caught and mirrored.

"Charmed," I said in response to their name. Eleanor squeezed my waist to keep from laughing. We picked up glasses of lemonade and sipped them on the periphery of the party. Margaret made my world large. Eleanor made it into a room only the two of us could enter. It was a room in which Eleanor kept her hand on the doorknob. I wished she wouldn't. I wished she'd forget about the door.

"I came in my sleep once," I said. I spoke in a low but not whispered voice, and I gave her a look that meant, *We're at a party, aren't we?*

She arched an eyebrow. "How did you know?"

"I woke up in a puddle," I said. "And the feeling."

Her expression writhed in answer. I waited for her to ask what I'd dreamed about, but she didn't.

"Now you tell me a secret," I said.

"What kind of secret?"

"The secret kind."

I thought maybe she'd tell me about Margaret. But then her mother saw us and called Eleanor away to speak to some friend of the family. I could have slid off to the bathroom to recover, but I didn't want to think about what I'd said. I hovered nearby in case Eleanor needed me as a reason to end a conversation, which meant that I myself became temporarily available to be approached by other guests of the party. They wanted to engage me in discussion about what they imagined my concerns to be. I had to tell more than one person that it was still too soon for me to know where I wanted to go to college. Some asked if I had a preliminary idea.

"No," I'd say. "No idea at all."

Because shouldn't they have known it was rude to ask me to identify my perception of my own intelligence through the prestige of whatever schools I might name? For what could they possibly do with the information except use it to form some opinion of me? Could I very well ask them what it was they thought they deserved?

"I actually don't have a favorite subject at school," I told a woman who was clearly making use of our conversation as an opportunity to reflect on some moment from her own life.

"I had this English teacher in high school . . ." she began.

But then, thank God, Eleanor reappeared beside me.

"Sorry," she said to the woman, and the woman accepted the word as an explanation for Eleanor leading me away, though in reality El had offered none. She took my hand, and this time we walked through the party as though on our way elsewhere and discouraged anyone from interceding by tipping our heads toward each other.

"My mom had an abortion when she was our age," Eleanor said, resuming our conversation.

I couldn't argue—this was a secret.

"Really?"

"Yeah."

"Is she okay?"

"Well, it's been a long time since then."

"Right." A warm August wind ruffled our hair from our shoulders.

"I mean yes. She had five kids after that. She had like the rest of her life after that."

"Did she tell you anything about it?"

"Only that it happened."

I thought of my hair, scattered in the garden. I thought of Eleanor's mom feeling afraid and uncertain. Neither seemed possible.

"Was it a girl or a boy?"

"I don't think she could know yet. Why?"

"I don't know." It was what I'd thought to ask. "I left my phone in your room," I said. "So we'd have a reason to go back."

"Like, genius."

We returned to the house through its back door. In the kitchen, a sweaty guest sat at the counter drinking an ice water. We moved quickly through the dining room, where Kim was in the middle of explaining a hole she'd cut in a wall to a group of admirers. We took the stairs two at a time, so we didn't hear the voices inside Eleanor's bedroom until we'd reached its door.

"You remember how small their old house was?" They were talking about a house Eleanor had never lived in. "From two bedrooms for four kids to this."

Eleanor went very still beside me. I put my hand on the doorknob. In her room stood a woman with her arm around the waist of a man. When they turned to face us, the man spilled some of his white wine.

"Shit," he said.

He held the cup away from his body to preserve his suit. Liquid dripped from his hand onto the carpet. Eleanor looked like she was about to pull a knife out of the air and gut these people, but the intruders missed her expression completely.

"Is this your room?" the woman asked. She seemed startled by our appearance but not embarrassed, as though we were all visitors to the museum of this house, merely arriving at different moments to appreciate a work of art.

"The door wasn't open," Eleanor said, but she said so quietly.

They didn't get it. The woman went on, "We were admiring all the effort your mom has put into this house. I would have loved a room like this when I was your—"

"You shut the door behind you," I interrupted, and waited for them to understand the possible interpretation of their behavior I was putting forward. Neither immediately moved. "This room belongs to a child."

Because compared to them we were children.

Finally, the woman turned red, not only her face but also her neck and shoulders. "Oh!" she said. "We weren't— We're so sorry."

While the man appeared to be still parsing my accusation, she yanked him out the door.

Eleanor looked me in the eye for one flaming second. I couldn't kiss her then, in the moment of her gratitude, because it would have implied a debt. Still, I gloried in having chased the trespassers away. You are who you are for all the people you love, at once. I was myself for my mother, completely. I was myself for Margaret, completely. But there was a person I could be for Eleanor that I'd never been before, and I now began to perceive her diamond silhouette, her sparkling hand on Eleanor's back. Eleanor ran to get a towel for the wine. I bent over my bag to retrieve my phone and felt beneath my pajamas for the edge of Eleanor's photograph. I'd brought it with me, a reminder to make me brave.

We ate dinner at the big tables set up in the backyard. The long light of summer hung on past eight, an open-ended dark blue against which the flames from the tiki torches trembled pale gold. Large white ceramic bowls of food with heavy wooden serving utensils were handed up and down the tables, eventually reaching me and Eleanor, seated all the way at the farthest end from her parents. The adults became drunk and exuberant, bordering on inappropriate. This kind of behavior from members of my parents' generation was unfamiliar to me, and I watched their revelry as a revelation. My own family was like an island, adrift and apart from other people. My parents' friends all lived in other states. They talked to our extended family over the phone and at holidays. I still thought the whole grown world, or at least most of it, was as serious and indomitable as my mother. No wonder El had such confidence, having seen for herself already that adults could be fools.

All through dinner we spoke to each other privately, with our chairs scooted very closely together, so that if our neighbors attempted to converse with us, they had to do so across obvious physical distance. I didn't feel bad for being rude, because Eleanor and I weren't really attending this party. We were an addendum, alone with each other but not alone at all, safe in our intimacy because of its limits. What a strange time of life—to be for the first time included in a larger social infrastructure but not yet subject to its rules or burdened by your own personal embodiment of its hypocrisy.

The catering staff carried out dessert, lemon tarts overladen with berries. Eleanor's father stood up at the end of the table and raised his glass, thanking everyone for coming to celebrate and thanking his wife for staying married to him all this time. The guests laughed.

"Our children are our joy," he said. The guests looked to us and applauded.

One of them stood up to thank the hosts and offer congratulations. The gaze of the party withdrew. While he spoke, his voice loud enough to carry down the long tables, Eleanor wedged her hand, palm up, beneath my thigh. He kept talking. She pushed further, steadily inward, until her fingertips met the hot space between my legs.

My eyes went hard as gems and my mouth fell open. She raised and lowered each finger one at a time, pressing my underwear into my flesh. Then she did it again. I looked at Eleanor, half mesmerized, half in disbelief, but she continued to face forward, toward the man still speaking at the other end of the table, not a line in her pixie face. She pushed harder on the keys of the instrument. I prevented myself from producing the notes of her song. When everyone raised their glasses, she withdrew her hand from beneath me and used her other to raise her own cup, to clink it calmly with her neighbor's. Then she turned and touched her glass to mine, which still sat on the table, dripping with condensation.

DINNER CONTINUED WITH MY BODY at an exclamation point. Again, Eleanor had identified a manner of advancing our relationship that allowed for no acknowledgment, bracketed as we were by the people sitting on either side of us and other social obligations, like the rest of dessert, which lasted long enough for me not to know how to bring us back to what she'd done. We spoke to our neighbors at the table. We ate our lemon tart. The party mostly ended by eleven. Eleanor and I traipsed in and out of the house, disassembling its components. Eleanor's father carried the final folding chair back down to the basement and excused himself to bed. Kim found one last guest lingering in the front hall. The woman, whom Kim called Nayan, explained she had to wait for the arrival of an unexpectedly distant rideshare, the nearest car still eighteen minutes away.

"I never remember to hit the request far enough ahead of time when I'm out here," Nayan said.

Kim waived off even the start of an apology. "Come keep us company in the kitchen while we do the dishes."

The plates, utensils, and glasses had all been rented, but the wooden and ceramic serving dishes, the elongated tongs, and stylish serving spoons all belonged to the house and had to be washed, dried, and returned to their shelves. I did the returning because I could reach all the high cabinets without a stepladder,

Eleanor instructing me where each dish belonged. Nayan took a seat at the raised kitchen island. She had long black hair oiled into a smooth wave and wore an incredibly chic olive-green column sheath that dragged on the ground a little bit when she walked. Her earrings were large gold shells. Of course Eleanor's mom's friends had good outfits.

Kim introduced me as "Mina, Eleanor's best friend," and Nayan as "my friend and orthopedic surgeon. She fixed my broken hand fifteen years ago, and then we started having lunch."

"I was going through a difficult breakup at the time," Nayan explained.

"And I had a broken hand, four teenagers, and a newborn baby," Kim went on. "She brought the lunch to our house."

Eleanor, who was drying a large ovular salad bowl, gave me a look that meant I was supposed to understand something about the situation that I didn't. They were telling their friend story to me, which wasn't something I'd received from adult women before, really.

Nayan offered to help with the dishes.

"When we've made it this far into the evening without breaking anything? Absolutely not," Kim replied. "Why trust a surgeon with my plates when I have two fifteen-year-old girls?" And then, noticing me and Eleanor standing the same way, both of us with our weight in one leg, hip out, she went on, "I remember when my friends and I all had the same mannerisms." Kim's teenage friendships had probably been much more similar to mine than my own mother's.

"Good Lord," Eleanor said, lifting up a giant wooden fork used to distribute salad. "Not a memory." Kim laughed. Eleanor continued, "Not my life, which I've lived this far only to prompt you to reminisce about your eight hundred friends and children."

Kim put a hand to her face, and Nayan began laughing too.

"How many lives have you lived through?" Nayan asked.

"Enough to find them all funny," Kim answered, her hands in the sink.

Nayan checked her phone for her ride's progress, and I felt a pang in my chest that she would be leaving. She was one of Kim's best friends—I could tell—but adults didn't have sleepovers. They didn't spend the night in their friends' beds and then wake up in the morning and eat cereal together. Instead, they went home. They saw each other once a month and made reports about their lives instead of living them together.

Eleanor sliced a handful of soap bubbles from the surface of the dishwater. She didn't throw the foam. That would have made a mess. Instead, she carefully placed the bubbles on top of her mother's head.

"Mmm," her mother said. "Thank you." And then she gently danced, so the foam tipped and jiggled but never fell. We all started giggling. When Nayan's ride arrived, Kim walked her to the door and kissed her on the cheek.

"You're a wonderful last person to have at a party. Overstay your welcome anytime," I heard her say. "And tell your wife we're sorry she was on call tonight and would love to see her soon."

However Nayan responded, I couldn't hear. She was the first woman with a wife I'd ever knowingly met. They were both doctors. I'd only met her for eighteen minutes, and I didn't say anything important or ask any questions. I didn't even get to see her wife.

UPSTAIRS, ELEANOR AND I PREPARED for bed without speaking. We washed our faces in her bathroom. The water she splashed on herself flecked my exposed neck and shoulder. I didn't remove my eye makeup. I felt like I still might require mascara. We got into her queen-sized bed and turned off the lights. Warmth emanated from Eleanor, the two of us lying back-to-back beneath a single sheet and her big cream quilt, the way we always did when we had sleepovers without Margaret. Eleanor knew Nayan had a wife.

I knew Eleanor and I wouldn't touch each other in her bed. Many times in the course of our friendship we had played video games at her desk until late at night and then slept like this. Eleanor bought and half-played games with abandon, whereas I wanted to finish every game I started. Sleeping in a bed together was sacred. We couldn't ruin it. We couldn't yet allow whatever was new between us to touch what already existed. It had to live where our friendship didn't, lest we lose the closeness we already had. Once we kissed in her bed, would we ever be able to sleep in it as friends again?

I couldn't sleep at all. I felt too aware of the bedsheets on my bare legs. I lay there for half an hour or more. I started thinking about Eleanor and Margaret kissing. I thought about Margaret's tongue in Eleanor's mouth. I thought about the face Eleanor made after she kissed me and wondered if now Margaret had seen it too.

A team of jealous horses frolicked and stomped on my heart. The worst part of Margaret and Eleanor kissing was that it aroused me. I didn't want them to have kissed each other in real life, but once they started kissing in my brain, I found it difficult to get them to stop. I wedged one hand high between my thighs to try to quiet my pulse there but then could think only of when the hand had been Eleanor's.

"Bea told me about Margaret," I finally said into the dark.

A long pause. "Don't say it doesn't matter because it was a dare," Eleanor said. Her voice didn't sound tired at all.

"I wasn't going to."

"Margaret doesn't appreciate—" She cut off. "You weren't there to kiss her instead of me. I didn't want to leave her alone in the moment."

"I know," I said. "I'm sorry."

I waited for an answer, but she gave none. She nestled further into the blanket. One of her feet brushed the back of my leg. I closed my eyes in the dark and waited to stop thinking.

In the morning, I packed my bag and was retrieved by my mother. I left the photo of Eleanor in a drawer in her bathroom with her face wash. I felt she'd given it to me on loan. I wanted her to know she could trust me to give her back to herself. Beneath the picture, I left her a note, handwritten on a sheet of the monogrammed stationery stacked on her desk.

I've never seen anything better in my life
hyperbole isn't good enough for you

A COUPLE OF DAYS AFTER THE PARTY, I WOKE UP VERY EARLY, WHICH wasn't like me, and walked downstairs.

"Mom?" I called.

She didn't answer. I heard the water running on the second floor, my father in his morning shower. I called again. I sometimes had dreams like this, dreams in which I walked the house, gradually checking the rooms where she most often sat—the kitchen, the living room, the bedroom—calling her name over and over again, louder, waiting for her annoyed answer of *Yes, I'm in here.* But the yes never came, and I kept calling her name until at last, I accepted that she was dead and woke up.

I looked out the window. On the front steps of the house, she sat with her coffee, staring into space. She wore a large denim jacket over her ankle-length nightgown. I opened the heavy front door and sat down on the stone step beside her. Neither of us wore shoes, the stone rough beneath our feet.

The sun was rising out of sight, beyond the trees that lined our block. Miniature pink clouds skipped across the sky above us, against a backdrop of fuzzy blue. Grass covered most of our front yard, though great flowering bushes lined the left and right perimeters of the property, almost completely obscuring the metal fence meant to divide the house from its neighbors.

"Those were only shrubs when we moved here," my mom said in a wistful voice.

I nodded, this being one of the statements about the house she made to me at least once or twice a year. Part of being an adult seemed to be the desire to repeat sentiments. This kind of repetition often roused my impatience. That morning, it made me tender. The tall plants created a sense of enclosure. I tipped my head onto her shoulder. I looked at her hands, her gold wedding and engagement bands, the watch with a gold face and brown leather strap on her wrist that she also wore every day. She turned and kissed my hair.

"I thought it would take you longer to start making trouble," she said.

"I feel like it took me a while," I responded.

"You're not very old."

"But I haven't ever made very much trouble either."

"You've made trouble," she said, and pressed the ceramic mug into her cheek. The steam from the coffee rose into her hair. "It scared me—already you're sneaking out into the night to kiss someone. You're sleeping somewhere other than where I thought you were. I thought you were in a specific bed, a couple of blocks away, where you've slept since you were six, but instead you were out in the world, exposed."

I could understand why that would be frightening. I remembered my mother's seeming indifference to the height of my emotion when we fought. Hearing how she'd really felt, even if I hadn't seen it at the time, the estrangement between us eased.

"I was okay, though," I said. Then I asked what I hadn't known I'd been waiting to ask. "Does it bother you that it's Eleanor?"

She drank some of her coffee and waited until she knew what she wanted to say. Her habitual and unapologetic slowness asserted that she was not obligated to understand herself right away or to answer to others on their clock. I often strained against it. In this moment, I felt suspense, but I also felt a higher order of trust in her wisdom that shielded me from really fearing her reply.

"No," she said finally. "It doesn't bother me that it's Eleanor. She's been a wonderful friend to you. It's hard for me to understand her mother's sense of security, but Eleanor does inspire confidence in her ultimate well-being. You can't help but believe that she knows what she's doing, except that she's still so young—as young as you are. It's unsettling at times for adults. Well, adults who notice that sort of thing. Though I thought she was like Margaret to you."

"So did I," I said.

"But they're not the same."

"No. They're not the same."

"I've been amazed your whole life about you and Margaret. I remember when you met, I didn't know you could talk so much. I think Nancy knew Margaret could talk that much, but she said she'd never seen Margaret want someone so badly as a friend." This was a story I'd heard before that I was glad to hear again. "After you met," she went on, "Margaret ran around the house asking her about everything, toys and clothes and dinner, *Does Mina like this?* Nancy said, *I don't know. You have to invite her over and ask to find out.* When I saw you and Margaret together, I felt like I had a better idea of the person you were going to turn out to be. It made me proud to be your mom, even though at times I was taken aback by your closeness. I didn't have a friend like Margaret growing up. I don't have any friends like that now."

"I'm sorry," I said.

"Yes, it's sad," she said, her voice even. "I sometimes feel very sad about it. You can't know how important and rare a friendship like that is. Your father wanted to move a couple of years ago, somewhere closer to his office, and I said we couldn't. We couldn't move you away from Margaret. You had to be able to walk to her house. It's unusual in life to live in walking distance of anyone you love."

I must have looked horrified, because she said, "I know," and stood up, her nightgown rustling at her ankles. She gazed out onto the street while she stretched, pushing her shoulders back and down and her chest up. I saw her close her eyes as she felt her body's extension. Then she turned around to face me again and continued.

"I don't dislike that it's Eleanor, but I worry about you because you're a tender heart. You were an extraordinarily honest child. It disarmed me, and your father. Even now, you have hardly any guile, whereas Eleanor, she understands how to conceal herself. That's not a criticism, and I'm not suggesting you learn to lie. Never have. But now, watching you become vulnerable like this—the way you have to, if you want to ask someone to love you—I'm reminded why other parents make other choices. I wish you had a little more armor, though I'm not sure where I expected you to get it."

I stood up to join her. We walked back into the house through the front door, which I'd left open. I followed her into the kitchen, where she emptied the remainder of her coffee into the sink, pulled the faucet head from its stem, and rinsed the trail of dark liquid down the drain. Then she put the mug in the dishwasher. I sat at the kitchen table, not in my usual seat because we weren't about to eat a meal. Instead, I sat in my father's seat, which faced the hallway toward the stairs.

"Eleanor," I began. I had to be careful. "She won't talk about being together." My mom considered this. She made a thinking noise. Now that we were in the kitchen, she began collecting miscellaneous dishes from the counters, which I tolerated. But when she made as though to wash one of them, I asked, "Do you really have to do that while we're talking?"

"No," she said, and walked away from the sink. She sat in the table's fourth seat, the one we left empty unless we had a guest, because that was the chair next to me. "You've tried to talk to Eleanor about having a romantic relationship, and she ended the conversation?"

"I mean," I said, "I've texted her. I've heavily implied." Had I left room for interpretation? I'd deleted everything. I remembered the strength of my sentiments but not the actual words I'd used.

"Eleanor might be afraid of changing the dynamic between the three of you."

"I thought so too, but she told Margaret about kissing me."

"She did?"

"Yes."

"Well."

"I agree, it means something."

She paused before replying. "You don't usually want me to speculate on the meaning of your friends' behavior," she said. This was true. I typically found whatever opinions she expressed upsetting. However, these were special circumstances.

"I don't have Margaret," I admitted, "to talk things through."

"Why not?"

"I didn't tell her about kissing Eleanor."

She gave me a look that meant she was finding something out about who I was as a person, and I flinched.

"I should have told her," I said.

"No, Mina," she replied, surprising me. "You don't owe your secrets to anybody. Margaret isn't the only person you're allowed to love. It's just unusual for you not to want to tell Margaret about something that happened to you, especially something good."

I put my chin in my hand, my elbow on the table.

"I told you, and it went badly."

I didn't know how to explain the effect of that first conversation. Eleanor had only very slightly kissed me. Then I learned that what happened between us could be made to feel even less by another person. The meaning of any event includes every time you've ever said it aloud. I couldn't risk putting the kiss into words again, not until I better understood what it meant between me and Eleanor, not until I believed in it enough to sequester the memory from other people's reactions.

"Mini," my mom said, which was what she called me when I was small. "I'm sorry how I reacted made you afraid."

I nodded. "I thought I would tell Margaret once I'd talked to Eleanor," I said, "once I knew for sure what was happening, but Eleanor—she never really acted like it was real."

My mother interlaced her fingers, her hands on the table, then asked, "Did that make you feel ashamed?" Who but your own mother can be so thoroughly unimpeded by your discomfort, so soberly discerning of your reality?

The answer was yes. Obviously, I'd wondered who I had to be for Eleanor to want me to be hers and say so. I'd kissed the mirror with my eyes open to try to see myself from the other side, but it's hard to make sense of your face with your nose to the glass. I'd kissed my inner arm many different ways to try to identify the best feeling, in case Eleanor gave me the chance to try again. I didn't want to be or act like someone other than myself, but I didn't actually know yet who I was in the context of wanting another person. Desire makes us new to ourselves.

"Afterward, I thought she'd want to"—I paused, then went

on—"claim me." I didn't want to ask my mom out loud what she thought I should do next, but then, I rarely needed to ask her a question for her to offer me the answer.

"Changing your relationship with Eleanor risks what you have with her and Margaret," she said. "It just does. All love is a risk. You risk who you'd be in its absence. I guess I don't feel ready for you to take risks. I don't want you to risk anything. I don't know if I ever will. But that doesn't mean that you shouldn't. Eleanor is very protective of herself. She's skeptical. She didn't really believe you and Margaret were her friends for at least a year after she began coming over here. Maybe she hasn't known how to proceed."

I asked her what she meant. She smoothed the patterned fabric of her nightgown across her thighs.

"None of you have any idea how to be with another person other than as a friend or a family member. If there's a way you want Eleanor to treat you, then you should show her what that is. If she can't or won't do it, then you have a problem. But there's always the possibility that she just doesn't know what else to do."

THOUGH MY MOM SAID IT was alright I hadn't told Margaret, her permission didn't make me feel better. In fact, over the next few hours, it began to make me feel worse. It pulled toward the surface certain problems whose shape and weight I'd felt and frightened me. I went for a walk. The air was heavy, laden with the promise of rain. I welcomed the humid weather because I liked to feel held closely by the atmosphere. I walked repeatedly around my own block and the blocks most adjacent.

When had I chosen not to tell Margaret? I thought I was waiting—for confirmation from Eleanor, for an opening from

Margaret. I thought the time that was passing didn't count as more and more days together, days in each other's digital and physical presence, in which I chose not to tell her this essential piece of information. I hadn't considered the decision made because it was a decision that undermined my sense of self, which for many years had been grounded in my relationship with Margaret and my faith in its total intimacy, the limits of which had only ever been imposed by her, not by me, or at least so it had seemed.

I approached a group of boys wielding lawn trimmers, long rods with rotating blades at the end. They walked up and down the tree lawns wearing their landscaping company–branded T-shirts, raising verdant clouds of cut grass. The whir of the blades put me at ease, the familiar summer sound layered over the thrum of cars passing and birds calling, the undercurrent of insects more audible in anticipation of rain. The boys would pause their machines to let me pass if I remained on their side of the sidewalk, so I crossed the street.

Margaret and I had hardly been alone together all summer until the night of the fair. No sleepovers just the two of us, not even any long conversations by ourselves on her porch. All that time and she hadn't asked me to explain myself, the way I usually insisted she fill in her own blanks once I became aware of them, before they took up too much space between us. Maybe once I'd started keeping the secret, she'd wanted to see how deep I'd dig the hole. Maybe she'd enjoyed the theatricality of having been wronged. Maybe she'd still wanted to give me the chance to tell her unprompted, and then I never did, not for weeks and weeks, not even in that booth having dinner, the two of us finally alone together and having what felt like a real conversation. Maybe she'd looked at me from across the table and waited for me to tell on myself, the way I always did, only to find that still I held my tongue.

I passed the boys with their lawn blades again, careful to cross the street. The smell of cut grass hung so heavy in the humid air it felt like I was breathing the vaporized lawns of the neighborhood into my lungs. Perspiration slid down my temples, between my breasts, behind my knees. Feeling porous and alive, I kept walking, beginning the circuit away from my house again, not yet done, not yet allowing myself to retreat.

The problem with talking to Margaret about Eleanor was that I'd have to use words, aloud. I didn't want to, and I didn't know how. Not the way Margaret talked to me about the boys she'd kissed. Not the way we always talked about everyone else on earth to each other, as though they were merely figures, as though they were representatives of themselves instead of people in their own right, as though Margaret and I were the only ones who were real.

Eleanor becoming our other best friend three years prior had complicated this dynamic with Margaret only somewhat. We loved and respected her. We treated our friendship with her as equal to our own, but also we didn't. In our heart of hearts, it mattered that she hadn't been there when we were children. She didn't borrow our clothes. She didn't sit around naked or get into the shower with us, a hesitance I now began to understand in a different light. This unspoken hierarchy of closeness had never led to a real impasse between the three of us because Eleanor held herself at a distance and because treating Eleanor as our additional best friend didn't challenge or impede the ways in which we'd always loved each other. But the way I felt about Eleanor putting her tongue into my mouth might.

I'd thought Eleanor was the one afraid of changing our friendship dynamic, but she'd told Margaret about kissing me, right away, and I hadn't. *All love is a risk,* my mom said. I hadn't allowed myself to contemplate how loving Eleanor might change loving Margaret, how I would manage what I owed to both of them, what I wanted to owe, to give, when I'd never done it before and when I had so little evidence of how girls could love each other, when I'd spent years thinking Haruka and Michiru were cousins, when Nayan was the first woman I'd met with a wife, and her wife hadn't even been there. I realized I had to start asking these questions I'd withheld from myself, because I wanted to date Eleanor, and I didn't know how.

I returned home, sweaty and smelling like myself. I put away dishes and swept the kitchen floor before ascending to my bedroom. I wanted my mom to feel justified in leaving me alone. I turned off my phone and read about sexually active fairies on my laptop.

Ginevra, having recently instituted complete peace and the ready availability of healthcare for her people, decided to leave her woodland territory for a brief trip. She wanted to visit one of her best friends and closest neighbors, Amphisbaena. She packed several diaphanous nightgowns, her pearl wand, and a special gift for her friend.

Whenever she left to pay such a visit, she found herself inevitably warned off by her people, even begged by them not to leave.

"Amphisbaena is known to be violent," her advisers pointed out.

"But she is not known to be treacherous," Ginevra countered. "She is only known to be capable of treachery, and the same could be said of any of you."

"But regardless of ill intent, we cannot hurt you," the advisers reasoned, for none of them possessed magic of Ginevra's ilk.

"Well, perhaps that is why I find Amphisbaena such an essential friend," Ginevra responded, and then flew off on lilac wing.

The reunited friends gallivanted through the stately gardens of Amphisbaena's court, speaking of all that had passed with each of them since their last meeting. Amphisbaena admitted that in a fit of disturbance she had cut off the hand of one of her lovers. She was still waiting for it to finish growing back.

"Oh, my dear," Ginevra said. "You must feel terrible. I hate whenever I accidentally dismember one of my loved ones on account of a mood. But I've brought something that will cheer you up."

She withdrew from her sack a scoop of very small beadlike blue mushrooms, native to her forest, and stuck them to the blades of Amphisbaena's collarbone. Luminescent blue tendrils began to extend from the mushrooms like veins across her chest.

"Stop!" Amphisbaena's advisers cried, as they leapt from their hiding place in a bush. They clamored to remove the glowing fungi from her body, but the mushrooms clung to her skin. The advisers turned with their shaking weapons raised at Ginevra.

"Oh, it's fine," she said, and stuck a handful of the mushrooms onto her own chest.

Their pale-blue fire spread until both Ginevra's and Amphisbaena's whole bodies glowed through their sheer nightgowns, their nipples dark blue and luminescent against the new night. Several of the advisers swooned to see their beauty and had to be recovered.

"I brought enough for all of us," Ginevra said.

And so there was a great revelry that night, the whole court dancing glow-in-the-dark through the gardens. In the morning, Ginevra and Amphisbaena celebrated their reunion by making excellent shared use of Ginevra's new pearl wand and then going to sleep for a month.

I pushed the hot computer off my stomach and writhed against my blanket until I found some half relief. Then I read the story again. At least I managed for a stretch not to think beyond these very narrow parameters.

Several hours later, my mom knocked on my door.

"Forget about me please," I said.

When I heard her feet retreating, I called, "I love you."

I WOKE UP IN THE MIDDLE OF THE NIGHT THAT NIGHT WITH MY mouth open and pushed a button on my phone. The screen came to life, revealing a banner with a message from Margaret she'd sent forty-five minutes earlier. She said she needed me to come and get her from Olivia's house. She wasn't in real danger, she reassured me.

i'm goood, the message said, *but if u see this.*

Olivia lived fifteen minutes on foot from my house, which meant she also lived roughly fifteen minutes on foot from Margaret's house, a distance Margaret had crossed more than once by herself in the middle of the night, even though when she'd told me she'd done so, I always gave her a look that meant she shouldn't have.

i'm coming, I responded, *stay where u are,* so she couldn't change her mind or decide she'd asked too much.

I woke my parents up by making a conspicuous sound when I opened their bedroom door and then putting a hand on my mother's shoulder, her skin hot from sleep.

"No one is dying," I began, "but I need to go get Margaret and bring her back here. She told her mom she's coming." If she hadn't yet, I'd make her.

My mom blessedly didn't ask me to explain. "Your dad will drive you," she said. Even in the middle of the night, you couldn't sneak up on my mother.

"No, he can't."

"He can drop you off at the end of the block, and you can walk up to the house by yourself."

I glanced at my phone—still no confirmation from Margaret. I refused to be discouraged. I was enamored with the idea of being needed by her.

"Fine, but I'm walking home with her. We're not getting in the car. And Dad can't talk to Margaret until tomorrow. Neither of you can."

The negotiation concluded, my father rose from bed in the dead of night without complaint in his matching suit of pajamas and put on the slippers he wore to get the newspaper from the end of the driveway in the mornings. He didn't say anything. He gave me a little pat on the shoulder that meant, *Alright.*

Olivia's house was the only one on her street with the lights on. Margaret sat on the lip of its open front door with mascara on her cheeks. I walked to her quickly. She took my hand when I offered to help her up. Neither of us let go once she was standing. She smelled like liquor. I'd never smelled alcohol on a person like that before. My parents hardly drank.

Through the front door, I could see into the living room and beyond that into the kitchen. Olivia sat on top of the counter with her arms crossed over her chest. Bea stood beside her, her eyes on her phone. At the last possible moment, Bea allowed her eyes to meet mine. We had an alliance when it came to Margaret, though neither of us knew exactly what the alliance was.

Margaret and I walked home in silence, holding hands. She didn't explain. I didn't apologize. Half a block ahead of us, my dad rolled slowly in his car. We didn't even laugh at him. Instead, we listened to the birds who still sang for each other in the unknown hours.

At home, I gave Margaret a pair of my pajamas even though she was already wearing her own. She took hers off and put mine on. We slept together in my bed. Her body blazed like a hot stone, heavy and solid on the mattress beside me.

IN THE MORNING, MY MOM looked very pleased to see the two of us descend the stairs. She handed me a house key attached to a tassel, and we left. A ten-minute walk brought us to the Metropark at the heart of Doan, a marsh enclosed by a steel weir plate. Through the marsh cut a wood-plank walkway with no railings. On either side of the path swayed living walls of marsh grass, bowed by the hot wind of an overcast morning. That late in summer, cloudy weather served as a sedative, and we found the park all but empty.

"I'm sorry I didn't tell you about Eleanor," I said. I'd been the one to take us apart from each other, by kissing our best friend, who had previously belonged to us equally, by wanting to kiss her more and then by allowing Margaret to find all this out from someone other than myself. I knew what I would have felt in the other direction: humiliated.

"You're supposed to be the one who tells the truth," Margaret said with real hurt in her voice and a confusion, too, at having been surprised by me.

"I know," I answered because that's who I'd been. "I'm sorry."

Margaret nodded. We both still wore our pajamas, braless, in flip-flops. The wind blew my shirt against and away from my bare chest in gusts.

"I kept thinking I'd tell you as soon as I knew for sure what was happening," I said. "Like if she never wanted to hook up again, I would have told you it happened the one time after I'd had a chance to recover. And if she wanted to make out all summer, I would have told you it was ongoing. But instead, it felt like neither. And the neither was horrible. Like intolerable. Like if I told you what happened, then I'd have to tell you what happened next—and what if nothing happened next? I've been waiting around to find out if Eleanor likes me, trying to act normal. If you'd been waiting too—it just felt too bad. But I'm sorry, and I've missed you."

This was all true, though its truth was partial, only as much as I could manage. Margaret listened without looking at me. The small hairs around her face whipped at her cheeks and forehead. The wood supports of the walkway had been drilled down into the marsh bed. Beneath the path grew great marsh grasses, six and eight feet tall, the water, that time of year, down at their ankles. In spite of my lifetime of visiting this marsh, my body still sharpened at the sense that, beyond a few planks of wood, between me and the water stood five feet of grass, of nothing, of air. Margaret took my hand and squeezed it.

"Liking El does seem hard," she said with sympathy.

"Does liking me seem easy?" I asked.

"For me," she answered. "But probably not for Eleanor."

Among the high grasses grew stalks of rose mallow, pale-pink heads of hibiscus that nodded and rippled in the gray wind.

"I can't believe she told you," I said. "I can't believe, after all that, you already knew."

"Why?" Margaret asked. Her voice became pointed. "Because she's only your best friend and not mine?"

"No. Because I thought she was ashamed of kissing me. I thought she wished it hadn't happened. She acted like it never happened."

"That's not true," Margaret shook her head. "Neither of you

ever acted like it never happened. I was there. You were both making severe googly eyes at each other the whole time."

"Oh," I said. "I'm sorry."

The idea of our attraction being legible from the outside made my heart flutter with pleasure and alarm. I wished I could have watched us myself, though I'm sure I would have cringed from the sight.

"It was mostly entertaining," Margaret said. "I'd never seen you do it before."

This was almost too much for me, Margaret spectating my behavior. I felt so much safer being the one watching hers.

"Tell me what happened last night," I said.

"Ugh, idiocy," she replied with an imperious roll of the eyes. "Total idiocy."

Margaret, I gathered, had grown fed up with her summer internship at the firm of Bea and Olivia, sick of being on the receiving end of the good fortune of being invited to join in other people's fun. She was fun! She instigated fun on Bea and Olivia's behalf before their desired audience of boys. Boys liked hanging out with Margaret without them. She had excellent cleavage. She'd been receiving text messages. She'd been liberally contouring her boobs all summer. It was already August, she reasoned, so if she pissed Bea and Olivia off a little bit, there wasn't all that much to lose. Lightly sloshed, Margaret had decided to reveal something impressive. Something to remind the troops of her sexual magnetism.

"I told them about the head-in-the-parking-lot situation," she said at my side. "Which I thought they would find salacious, given how often we go drink in this boy's basement."

It was like Margaret to make an admission to me in this way—telling me something in the middle of telling me something else more interesting so I couldn't interrupt. But I didn't miss it, what they'd been up to.

Margaret had been ready to be admired. She'd been ready for a little sporting jealousy.

"Unfortunately, Olivia had already been boning him for weeks."

"What!" I said. "I'm sorry—what?"

She nodded with ironic solemnity.

"Full-on sex?"

"Full-on sex. Penetration. P in V."

The arrangement of the information was funny—Margaret always made it funny—but she looked away from me after speaking.

"I know," she said to whatever she imagined I was thinking.

We passed a woman and her child out for a walk and hoped they hadn't heard us. I spoke more quietly.

"Did you know?"

Margaret crossed her arms and kept walking. "How could I have known? She never told me."

"No, but you knew," I said, realizing that she had.

She sighed. "I didn't know they were having sex. I didn't know they were hooking up. I obviously would not have spontaneously announced that I sucked his dick if I knew that."

But as she said so, I gave her a laughing look, because some part of Margaret's personality definitely would have loved to make that announcement.

"Lol, that would have been very hardcore of me," she said. "No—but I did think maybe she was into him."

"And his friends," I stopped walking to say, "dared him to kiss Olivia when they had the chance." But Margaret kept walking. This wasn't evidence she wanted to consider. "Well, none of that was evil of you," I said. "We don't have to pretend it's not fun to hook up with someone that other people also find attractive." Margaret compulsively took her phone out of her pocket and then put it back again. She sped up a little. I had to quicken my step to keep pace.

"It's messed up you thought you didn't have to tell me about kissing Eleanor because you thought Eleanor wouldn't," she said, returning the conversation to me.

"It's not like you tell me every time someone rejects you," I countered.

"El didn't reject you."

"She left me on read for weeks."

"It's Eleanor! You think she's going to say she likes you via text message? You think she's going to, like, etch her feelings for you into stone because you kissed one time?"

"Fair."

I had considered this, but I believed it more coming from Margaret. The wood-plank path widened into a lookout point Binoculars had been soldered to a metal rod. We stopped to watch a blue heron lift off a log in flight.

"And Bea really let Olivia kick you out?" I asked, worried I wouldn't be able to explain my secrecy about Eleanor if Margaret pushed further. "She should have stood up for you," I said.

Margaret shrugged. "She knows she doesn't have to." Whatever happened, Bea would still be Margaret's cousin, whereas Olivia was only her friend.

"And you're okay with that?"

"I mean, I get it."

I wanted to protest that she shouldn't get it, that she wasn't obligated to be understanding about Bea's behavior, that I'd never have done the same, that I'd never have abandoned her like that, even if she'd done something wrong, for the sake of preserving someone else's feelings—except that I didn't know that anymore. I didn't know what I'd do if she hurt Eleanor. We sat down on the park's single bench. The plaque on its backrest dedicated the seat to a dead woman. Margaret pushed her hundred bracelets up and down her wrist.

"Why hadn't you told them already?" I asked.

"I was waiting for a fun time."

"You mean you didn't think they'd invite you out with them if they knew you had a head start?"

Margaret allowed my interpretation to stand.

"Pun," she said, with a point of the finger at me, which I waved away.

"How much were you texting him?"

"A medium amount," she said.

"Still? Recently?"

She slid a breezing piece of hair behind an ear. "Not unrecently."

"Are you sad?"

"Somewhat," she said.

I wrapped my arms around her and put my chin on her head.

"I'm sorry, bb," I said. "Should we go throw a tomato at him?"

"Ugh, maybe," she said. "I honestly would feel better about it if I could feel worse. Like if we hooked up yesterday and then I found this out, it would be a betrayal. But instead, we hooked up two months ago, and then he began a new thing, and then I told people about it yesterday like it was still important to me."

We sat for a moment in silence, sweat on our skin, wind on our faces.

"You know El gave me a physical, printed-on-a-piece-of-photo-paper naked picture of herself by putting it in my purse and never telling me?"

Margaret's sadness, her vulnerability, called forth the same from me. Margaret nodded.

"Like, what was I supposed to do with that?"

"Well, you could have sent her one back."

"No. I couldn't have. We all know I couldn't have."

"Both of you are obsessed with being in control of what happens."

"I'm not," I protested. "El is. Am I?"

Margaret was my most essential witness to myself. No one else could tell me who I was like she could—not my mom, who read me inevitably as her daughter—and I'd deliberately prevented Margaret from doing so.

"Eleanor likes to fuck around, but precisely, like in a precise manner of her choosing, in order to find out what happens as a result—" Margaret began.

"That's controlling," I interrupted her to say.

"That's Eleanor's version of controlling," she corrected me before continuing. "You never want to fuck around in the first place."

"I fuck around," I said defensively.

Margaret rolled her eyes. "You absolutely do not," she said. "You try to think all the way through what would happen if you did and then skip over actually having to do it. One of the eighty text messages you sent El was a picture of a leaf."

She'd seen my text messages?

"That was such a cool leaf though," I protested. It had been bedewed and reticulate, veins radiating delicately across its green surface.

"She showed you her boobs!"

"Not yet she hadn't!"

Margaret waved away my objection to chronology. We laughed. I took her point.

"So you're saying a leaf covered in tiny drops of water isn't an equivalent offering to showing someone your naked body? These are the mistakes I make when you're not available to instruct me," I joked, but I did yearn for her instruction, for the possibility that she knew how I should behave and would tell me, or at least that we could figure it out together.

Margaret shoved me a little. "You know you don't have to worry about me and El kissing, right?" she asked. "We don't want to hook up with each other. It was just our mouths touching."

"Don't say that," I responded, remembering in that moment that Margaret had hurt Eleanor, and that I did have to do something. I had to at least make sure Margaret understood. "That's why El is mad at you—for acting like she didn't do you a favor by kissing you in front of a bunch of people, for acting like two girls kissing doesn't mean anything when you know it does to her."

"El is mad at me?" Margaret asked, and sighed. "Of course if El's mad, she has to get mad in secret."

"You were mad at me in secret," I pointed out.

"It wasn't a secret. You knew I was mad at you, and you still didn't fix what you'd done wrong."

I felt strangely proud of Margaret for saying this and grateful because with other people she might have hurried away from the conflict, but with me she kept pointing out what I'd done wrong, the inconsistencies in my logic, and this was how I knew she wanted to forgive me and believe it.

"I didn't really know you were mad at me," I said. "I thought maybe you just wanted new friends."

Margaret shook her head. "I like hanging out with lots of people, but none of them are you and me."

"No," I said. "They're not."

She sighed. "I sent him such a dramatic text message," she said. Then she stood up and tossed her phone into the marsh.

"Margaret!"

"What?" she said.

She started laughing. I started laughing. Then she started crying, and the invisible life of the marsh—the birds and frogs and bugs and fish—rose up to join her in keening. I wiped the tears from her cheeks, and we took a picture of ourselves on my phone, for posterity.

I COULD HAVE BEEN ANGRY AT MARGARET FOR GETTING DRUNK without me. Instead, I decided to catch up with her. We gathered at Eleanor's house, the best place for hooliganism given its size. I didn't want to get drunk for the first time in a basement with a bunch of people I only medium liked looking at me, and I didn't want to get drunk for the first time in the back of a car and hope the driver would keep their word on sobriety. I didn't want total chaos. I wanted chaos without risk. I wanted to be stupid without being worried. I wanted to be foolish but not a fool, or be a fool but only in the company of my best friends and for a limited amount of time and without consequence.

We ate dinner with Eleanor's parents at their oblong dining room table, vegetables and fish. Afterward, we made a big show out of watching a movie, and when the movie ended, we went upstairs and played music at a volume sufficient to mask our conversation and deter awareness of any odd sounds we might make. Unlike at my house, where my mom would have stuck her head around my door and asked that we turn down the music, Eleanor's parents retired to their bedroom and left us alone.

We skipped around in circles trying on clothes. We crowded into Eleanor's bathroom, which was pale blue and pristine, its countertops empty until Margaret and I spilled our million cosmetic items onto the granite. I began my makeup application rather gleefully. I was getting what I wanted, a collective first time, and ignoring what I didn't yet know how to resolve. For the rest of our lives, we'd live in each other's first memory of drunkenness. Margaret had pinky-sworn to feign ignorance for the sake of the team.

We were still giddy from our reconciliation, high on again being able to send each other text messages about what we'd eaten for breakfast. In the group chat, too, we bantered, sent links to the behavior of other people on social media for discussion. Eleanor chimed in occasionally, reserved. Because I hadn't seen her in almost a week and because Margaret and I hadn't said Eleanor's name again between us since I apologized for keeping the secret, it felt possible to pretend for an evening that I knew how to behave hanging out with both of them at the same time, the three of us together. I used shimmering green eyeliner to trace the rim of my eye.

"You're not going to immediately tell your mom about this, are you?" Eleanor asked while brushing her hair, which I found both rude and flirtatious.

Obviously, I didn't like doing something to which, had I asked her permission, my mother would never agree. However, I thought if she accepted the premise that I had to get drunk now and not later, not all the way in the future when it became legal and everyone else had been drinking for years, then she would have found my approach reasonable. I knew she would have preferred that I get drunk for the first time by drinking wine in our living room, both parents present, but I had to try to be at least the smallest amount interesting. I had to endeavor to be the least bit cool.

"Nope," I said, flippantly and without looking her in the eye. The last time I'd seen Eleanor she had driven a hand beneath my dress. I'd prepared myself for sleeping in the same room as her again by masturbating repeatedly earlier in the day.

"Good," she answered, but she hardly seemed excited for the night's events. She and Margaret hadn't seen each other since the fair. "We don't actually need to get ready for this," she said.

Margaret scoffed, as if getting drunk for the first time wasn't obviously an event that merited hair and makeup. As if we weren't always practicing how to be beautiful for the rest of our lives.

"You're wrong," Margaret said, staring at her face in the mirror with a liquid eyeliner pen in one hand. "I need winged eyeliner. I have a vision of myself being drunk with winged eyeliner on. That way, if I cry, I'm a sad queen."

"Why?" Eleanor asked with her hands in the sink. She always washed her hands before she touched her face. She patted her wet palms on the pale blue hand towel that hung from a silver ring. "Are you planning to cry?"

"I mean, I might," Margaret answered, holding down one of her eyelids and contemplating where first to apply the pen. She didn't say she'd cried the last time, though I knew she had. "Especially if I'm wearing the right eyeliner."

I held a hand above my plugged-in straightener to test its heat. I straightened and then released the first section of my hair. It fell silkily upon my shoulder. Silky hair sensations are helpfully productive of confidence, and I wanted confidence.

"I wonder if I'll throw up," I said.

"You're definitely going to throw up," Eleanor said. "Accept it now."

"Great, thank you."

Margaret made an initial stroke of ink on her eyelid and then immediately regretted it.

"Do you have makeup remover?" she asked Eleanor. And then, "Mina, you're not going to throw up. I'm not going to throw up. No one is going to throw up. Throwing up is forbidden because it's gross."

"But if you do throw up," Eleanor said, "please do it quietly."

She sounded resentful. Margaret reassuring me had irritated her. Eleanor must have heard her control over her tone of voice slip too, because she left the room in pursuit of makeup remover, which I was sure she kept beneath her bathroom sink. When Margaret likewise departed to fetch a hair tie from her bag, I quickly opened the drawer in which I'd left El's photo. Neat rows of skincare filled the drawer, products organized by category within clear Lucite dividers. Both the picture and my note were gone. All the bottles had been rotated, so their labels faced forward. I stared at the drawer's contents for a moment. Then I turned a few of them around.

After an hour of further preparation, we deemed ourselves sufficiently sparkled. Margaret sprayed a heavy cloud of perfume into the air. Eleanor and I ran through it with our eyes closed, our chests thrust forward, and our heads thrown back like beautiful vegetables being misted at the grocery store.

Eleanor slunk up and down from the basement by herself. We'd agreed on this as the least conspicuous course of action. She took a picture of the large wooden bar built into her basement's back wall so that she could reassemble the bottles afterward exactly as they'd been.

"Genius," I said when she explained this to us, and she gave me a look that meant, *Obviously.*

Then she carried bottles up the two flights of stairs to her bedroom in a tote bag she'd lined with a fleece blanket to prevent the glass vessels from clinking against each other. Eleanor loved being logistically prepared for mischief, which I found charming, though I also felt wary of her mood, which she'd hidden again.

On her desk, we lined up disposable mouthwash cups, the tiny vessels decorated with finely drawn mint-colored flowers, which, in my emotion about our forthcoming rite, I found beautiful. Into each cup, El poured a small draft. In the first, an inch of vodka, the next, an inch of whiskey, then wine, and last grenadine, none of us aware the red liquid didn't actually contain any liquor.

This finished, Eleanor carried the bottles back downstairs, returned them to their original locations according to her photograph, and carried up four more. She continued up and down the stairs until we felt confident she'd siphoned enough liquid to get three teenage girls drunk but not so much as to be noticed by her parents. I think El was pretending her parents were very observant and scrutinizing of her misbehavior. A little superstition enhances experience.

As we drew closer to the actual consumption of alcohol, I felt increasingly uneasy. I didn't know what was about to happen to me. I sat down on the floor.

"No dying tonight, okay?" Eleanor said as she walked out of her bedroom to return the last of the bottles.

Margaret rolled across the carpet like a log to reach me.

"You make the most insane faces—like absolute looks of despair in her direction," Margaret said. Reading my nerves, she added, "This is going to be fine. You'll be fine."

"I won't turn into someone else, poof?"

She pushed her stack of bracelets high up her wrist. "Nope, I promise," she said.

"You didn't turn into someone else?" I asked.

"You mean I've been drunk before? Gasp."

I rolled my eyes at her posturing. I wanted to be reassured before Eleanor got back and saw that I needed more reassurance. Margaret propped her head up with her hand, her elbow against the floor.

"No," she said. "I didn't turn into another person. I was me, just a little more willing to be an idiot. I felt a lovely desire to say whatever occurred to me."

"Don't you already do that?"

"Like yes, but usually there's at least a second of resistance. People use alcohol as an excuse to be different than who they are because who they are is boring. My mom told me that. You already say weird things. You'll be fine."

I put one of my feet on her thigh.

"What about El?" I asked. "Will she still be El, or different?"

"I guess we'll find out," Margaret said as Eleanor walked back into the room. We hadn't heard her feet on the stairs or her hand turning the doorknob.

"What are you trying to find out about me?" she asked, and, for a moment, I thought she looked afraid.

"Whether or not you'll turn into a two-headed serpent after drinking this magic potion," Margaret answered smoothly.

"I mean, hopefully I will," Eleanor said. "Will you?"

"It seems likely," Margaret answered, and slithered suggestively on the floor. "This is what snakes do, right?"

I raised my miniature cup in salute, and they raised theirs. Then we all drank and appeared humbled by the taste. I'd made the mistake of taking a test sip of my vodka first and felt my organs shudder and chastise me. However, I was determined to make use of my rule-breaking—having come this far, I couldn't fail to actually get drunk—and so consumed the rest of the liquid in a single swallow and followed it as fast as possible with orange juice. Margaret did a little panic dance as though she'd drunk the whole thing, but I saw the second half of her shot still sitting in her cup. And Eleanor knocked her drink down in one gulp but then looked like she didn't know if it was coming right back up. Then we sat around on the floor, waiting to be transformed.

I'd never been influenced by anything but a high fever until that night. I thought I'd know the minute alcohol made a change in me, the moment I felt like anything other than myself. We grew impatient with the lack of results and drank more thimbles of liquor. We took pictures of ourselves on the floor of Eleanor's bedroom, hanging upside down off the edge of her bed, positioning our lips to maximize our cheekbones, and absolutely believing they were the best pictures we'd ever taken in our lives. But these were all activities we'd do at a regular sleepover, and I failed to notice a shift in the urgency of my thinking. I did feel a frisson in the distance between myself and Eleanor, like a plucked nerve. I thought—I knew—she felt me thrumming from the other side.

"I hope we have every first together for the rest of our lives," I said extravagantly. "No one is allowed to smoke weed or have a baby without me."

"That's a little unreasonable," Eleanor responded, as though I'd really meant it, because in fact I had.

"Well, I'm an unreasonable woman," I said, because I wanted to grow up to be one. I noticed that my voice sounded angry. What I felt was thrilled because Eleanor took my flippant remarks seriously, because she heard the truth in my frippery. Her graphite eyes defied mine.

"If you're going to be so loud," she said imperiously, "I think we should go outside." She got up and left the room without checking whether or not we'd follow. Margaret looked at me, as though expecting explanation, and I shook my head.

At night, the pool made a dark lake. Margaret sat down at its edge and put her legs in the water. Eleanor kept walking, and I went after her. Low, illuminated metal lamps lined the paths of the garden, which were paved with stones set deeply into the earth. I felt their rough caress beneath my bare feet. Eleanor walked on tiptoe to the end of a path flocked by the shadows of great leaves. She pivoted on raised feet like a ballerina to face me, then lowered down onto her heels slowly, with deliberate control.

"We don't have to do every single thing together," she said with her shoulders back and her posture sewn up tight. "We're allowed to be our own people."

Her tone was haughty. She sounded like she was mad at me, but alcohol dulled my ability to feel immediate alarm. Instead, I felt aroused, being alone with her and receiving such a deliberate look. I liked that she was accusing me of something. An accusation is a kind of claim.

"I know we don't, but isn't it more fun this way?" I said and smiled, a little stupid, fizzing with love for Eleanor being who she was, so private and a little violent, for her elfin face and gray eyes, her high cheekbones and pink mouth, for her hotness, which I seemed to have spent years trying not to fully notice but which alcohol blazed upon me in potent clarity. It occurred to me that I'd never once seen her eat a lollipop, and this seemed a shame. Eleanor turned her face over her left shoulder, and I admired her profile, the line of her nose, her pointed chin. She impatiently exhaled. She didn't want me to smooth the serration of her mood. She'd been waiting to tell me something, I realized.

"Like yes, I'm having a good time," she said, and then after a brief pause, "but I've been drunk before."

"What?" I said, a lag between what Eleanor was telling me and what I understood. "With who?"

She rolled her eyes. "With no one. By myself."

"You promised," I said, indignant, like I still thought she could be wrong.

"You made us promise," Eleanor said. "You put us on the spot and literally insisted that we promise. What was I going to say—no?"

"Yes. You could have said no, obviously. Then it wouldn't have been a promise you made me." Heat flooded my face, seeped into my chest. I told myself I wasn't allowed to cry, because this was a stupid thing to cry about. Still my cheeks got wet, and I wiped them away. I knew that by the standards of other people, she was right—that it was a weird or at least unreasonable thing to get this upset about—but the standards of other people didn't matter. They were less than us, and she should know that. "So you literally lied to me just to get me to go away? You gave me your word, and you never even planned to keep it?"

One of Eleanor's legs had begun to tap up and down an inch impatiently. "I didn't like write you a letter in blood, Mina. All I did was say okay when you asked for something and then later change my mind."

I breathed in, and my throat felt narrow. "You're wrong," I said. "Stop acting like nothing we do to each other matters."

"Margaret's been drunk before." She shot this at me. Did she know about Margaret getting kicked out of Olivia's house, or had she been present for those other unnamed nights Margaret had alluded to but not explained? I remembered Eleanor standing above me while I swam in her pool after the Fourth, deliberately reassuring me that they hadn't gotten drunk in my absence. She'd wanted me to know that she kept her word. "You're fine pretending for Margaret. Did she even apologize to you for breaking her promise?" Eleanor held her chin high. "Of course not. Of course you skipped that part and forgave her anyway."

Here, this was what she'd wanted to tell me, to force me to acknowledge. This was what I'd done: become friends with Margaret again, gone backward toward who we used to be, the three of us, made an exception for Margaret's behavior in my eagerness to resume our friendship, like I always did, that I wasn't willing to make for Eleanor, or at least, caught off guard, that I wouldn't make for her immediately.

"When did this happen?" I asked.

"I don't know. A couple of days ago." So, after I'd told her we were all about to get drunk together.

"What was the point of that, to hurt my feelings?"

"No! Mina, God. I just like doing things by myself, especially when it's for the first time."

That was a lie or at least a blind. She'd done it to make a point. She'd done it so she could accuse me like this, so she could yell at me, and I'd have to answer, which meant she wanted me to answer. She wanted me to treat her differently, and this was the way she'd found to say so. Anger and betrayal began to drain away in favor of understanding.

"You know how things are with Margaret," I said in a conciliatory tone. Eleanor was the one to whom I complained, the one I invited over to receive my frustrations before I put them all aside and acted like they hadn't happened. She was sick of it.

"Yes, I do know," she said, and swayed a little on her feet. "This is exactly the position I didn't want to be in."

"What position?" I took a step down the path toward her, plants shoulder-high on either side of me, the moon in the sky.

She exhaled angrily, and I thought I heard a catch in her breath. "Margaret demonstrating oral sex on you and me wondering if you'll ever like me as much as you like her!"

I couldn't believe she'd said it. I felt like Sailor Moon with the power of the planets beaming down into my naked rainbow body. I closed the rest of the distance between us, so I stood directly before her, looking down on her face from above. In her eyes, I saw tears. She blinked at them. A droplet of water clung to her pale lashes.

"It's not about how much. It's about what kind, what way." I picked up her hands from her sides and held them. They were smaller and colder than mine. They were delicate. "You don't have to wonder," I said. "I love you."

I spoke without thinking. Everything Eleanor had done to hold me at a distance suggested that she wasn't a person who wanted to receive a proclamation of love or be expected to respond to one, that she hadn't responded to my text messages because she knew that given the slightest opportunity I was a person who would say too much, who would deliver my heart on a platter after having been kissed only one time.

Yet I could see that I'd said what she wanted to hear. A perfect vulnerability came over her features, that same expression I'd only ever seen once before, right after she kissed me on the field. It was an expression of intense hope and yearning. "I won't say it again until you ask me to," I told her, in a whispered voice. She nodded quickly, her eyes on mine, so I'd know this was right. "And I won't tell anyone else I've said it at all," I promised, keeping still my eyes on hers, so she'd understand what I meant and who I wouldn't tell. "It's just yours, for only you to know and keep."

"Yes," she said, like that was all she could get out. Then she took her hands from mine and slid them around my waist. Clasping me tight, she pressed her brow against my chest. I felt her tears wet my skin. I closed my arms around her in a kind of embrace I'd never known before, so closely and completely did our bodies align, her breasts below mine, pressed against my stomach.

"Will you be my girlfriend now?" I asked, still quietly but above a whisper because I had to be sure she heard me. She nodded into my chest. We didn't kiss. We just stood there in each other's arms for as long as we could manage, and then we stepped away. We were still too new for more. I felt overjoyed and wrung out, like I wanted to go to sleep before my life had the chance to become any less perfect than it was right at that moment. We walked back to the pool and found Margaret prostrate. When she tried to sit up, she melted back down sideways.

"Mina is my girlfriend," Eleanor announced to neither of us, to both. An enormous bursting pride shivered through me. I grinned and blushed and grinned.

"Yay!" Margaret said.

Then a glaze came over Eleanor's face, and she threw up in a bush.

"This happened to me last time too," she moaned, standing up. Then she spit into a pit of flowers. We all laughed, and I brushed back Eleanor's hair. Then we helped Margaret to her feet, and she wrapped her arms around us. Her body felt heavier than I expected, the way she clung to our shoulders.

NOT LONG AFTER OUR INAUGURAL INEBRIATION, ELEANOR INVITED me to her house by myself. I rode over on my bike. I didn't want to have to be dropped off by my mother at an appointment to hook up with my girlfriend. In my head I kept saying the word *girlfriend*. I was someone's girlfriend. I'd never been one before, not really, and the thought of being one now made me giddy, aroused, also slightly terrified.

I had no idea what being Eleanor's girlfriend entailed. Would she invite me over by myself like this a lot? Would she want to hang out with me alone as much as we hung out together with Margaret? Would I need to spend less time overall with Margaret in order to spend more time with Eleanor because there was a limit to the amount of my life my mom would allow me to allocate to people who weren't my family? A block from Eleanor's house, I took off my helmet, shook out my hair, tried to peel my shorts from where they'd stuck to my thighs, and exhaled a few times.

When I arrived, we struggled to make conversation. The emotion and spectacle of our last exchange seemed impossible to resume. What could follow? I cringed from every idea. Those girls in the garden that night didn't seem like they could have been us, not Eleanor, walking up the stairs to her bedroom almost on her tiptoes, not me either, walking one pace behind her, gangly and silent, my gaze down, watching her white ankle socks rise step by step.

Eleanor opened her bedroom door and closed it behind me. This action alone was enough to embarrass us both intensely. Eleanor's skin turned pink. The pale hair on her arms looked slightly raised. I avoided eye contact, just followed as she marched to the far side of her bed and sat down on the ground. I realized, from the position she'd chosen, that we wouldn't be visible right away to anyone who unexpectedly opened the bedroom door, which meant she'd been thinking about how to do this. She'd made a plan.

My bare legs sank into the plush carpet. The half-inch inner seam of my denim shorts—hard, overlapping fabric—drove an upward vector between my thighs. I shifted, not to relieve the position, but to more exactly align the seam against myself. Now that we'd arrived here, at her chosen location, I saw that Eleanor didn't know what to do next. She could initiate no further under these circumstances, not face-to-face in daylight with no obvious means of curtailment or escape. She didn't know how to tolerate vulnerability as a continuous state.

Even though we'd just sat down, she looked like she was about to find a reason to get up again. Her thighs were pressed together, and she pushed her hands down the crevice between them, palm to palm, rather than sit still. I could feel her over there itching to either make out with me or ruin our relationship. I knew she must have had all the same questions I did and less patience for them. I needed to reassure her that we could forgo any acknowledgment of our own past behavior, before I became yet another threatening Sim she decided was easier to drown in the pool than play with.

"Hi," I said, to start a new moment. Searching for what to say next, I wondered if you were supposed to warn a person who might be about to touch your boobs when one of them was bigger than the other one. Then I realized I didn't have to tell Eleanor, because she was my best friend and already knew. The resulting wave of relief made me brave, so I kissed her, at first awkwardly, with my mouth open, but then passionately, as she met my gestures with just as much eagerness. She licked my tongue with her tongue to tell me don't stop, don't be discouraged by how strange this is—because of how wonderful the strangeness was, a strangeness that was both of our faults and therefore neither's.

We shone with our mutual intention to please each other. I felt Eleanor's determination, the same as mine, to put away shyness after having made it so far. Perhaps we were also afraid of what would follow stopping, of what would come next when we had no idea. Instead, we found each other as we went, as we kissed and kissed. Eleanor at first firmly held my hands by my sides, like she wanted to be sure of what I was doing with them. I remained still, and she gained confidence. She slid a hand into my underwear and began to stroke me.

I couldn't instruct her aloud in what would feel good, and I felt alone in the performance of being touched. So I did what she had done and slid my hand beneath her dress. That way at least we were equally in the unknown. I found her soft and wet. I did to her what I thought I might like her to do to me. Our heads drooped against each other, her hot cheek against my chest, my face against her shoulder. Every so often one of us would nod slightly, either to tell the other they'd done right or because we couldn't help it.

We continued until we stopped. We didn't know how to arrive

at the place where our bodies were urgently directing us to go. Still, it felt like a revelation to place my hand assuredly on the soft inner bend of her waist and know that I could keep it there. When we were finished kissing, we lay on the floor facing each other.

Eleanor wrapped a strand of hair around her index finger, then unfurled it. Only in retrospect would I understand the fear and discomfort that held Eleanor back that summer. Desire is an impingement on interior life, and Eleanor held her interior life sacred. Intimacy requires or else produces true presence within yourself in front of another person, and Eleanor preferred to occupy herself in private. She liked to know herself ahead of being known by other people, and there I was, loving her well enough to watch in real time the cursor of her personality blink against its blank page, to watch the next line in the code of herself as it was being written. There I was, catching her in the present act of being herself. But she had less complicated fears too.

"Why didn't you tell Margaret about us kissing?" she asked.

I felt awash in the possibilities implied by the question. I took her right hand in my left.

"Were you sad I didn't?"

"Well, I thought you would," she said, looking down at our hands, allowing them to remain where they were, not trying to part them. An interpretation of my behavior that had never occurred to me before occurred to me then.

"You mean you thought—so this girl can send me a million text messages, but she won't tell her best friend we kissed?"

Eleanor shrugged, visibly embarrassed but also inching closer toward me, like I was protection from my past self. "Yeah, kinda."

I shifted closer too, so our feet touched through our socks. "I'm sorry," I said in a soft and dear voice. I felt honored by this new confidence, this requesting of an apology. I felt moved that she would acknowledge I had hurt her for the sake of allowing me to wash it away. I explained how sincerely I'd thought she would want me to treat the kiss as a secret and then how later I'd feared she might wish it had never happened, but I acknowledged that these weren't the only reasons.

"The truth is," I said, "I don't know why completely. I've been trying to understand myself. I think I didn't want to hear what she thought. I didn't want her to have a response to it. I felt possessive about the memory. I thought she'd be like, *But we've kissed before, and we don't want to hook up.* I thought she might make me feel like what happened between us wasn't real, and I was the only one who thought it was."

"That's what you worried?"

"That's one of the things I worried."

Eleanor nodded. "I can tell you she didn't respond that way. She gave me a hug and asked if you were a good kisser."

I felt proud of Margaret for having this response to Eleanor's disclosure and ashamed of myself for being too afraid to receive the same, but I also knew that Eleanor wasn't me, and Margaret wouldn't say the same things to Eleanor that she'd be willing to say to me. "How did you reply?"

"I said I was better."

"Rude!" I said, and kissed her again.

Eleanor changed into a pair of soft shorts and a long-sleeved T-shirt and no bra beneath instead of putting back on her dress.

"Won't that be like a little conspicuous?" I asked, sitting up.

She needed a moment to understand what I meant. "Oh, no one notices anything around here," she said.

As we walked down the stairs, I felt the old distance between us returning. Our good faith lingered, but the transparency between us couldn't. Eleanor's goodbye was oddly formal.

"Thank you for having me over," I replied in kind, stupidly, but I also touched her arm in reassurance. We'd done well, I wanted her to know. We didn't have to do everything at once. We'd used up our courage and were tired and needed to recover by ourselves before we could start again.

MARGARET CAME OVER THE NEXT DAY TO HEAR MY REPORT ON HAVing a girl's tongue in my mouth. We ran up the stairs to my room. Summer's heat had mellowed. I had all my windows open, and the wood-slat ceiling fan circulated lazily. Margaret had told her mom her phone fell out of her pocket into the marsh. Nancy accused Margaret of having lost the phone on purpose for the sake of getting a new one. Margaret could have gotten into real trouble for this, but instead she pointed out that her mom could be the one to get the new phone, and Margaret could inherit her mom's old one.

"She loves when I'm the reason she has to buy something new for herself," Margaret said, and tossed the new old phone onto my bed, where it made a divot in the center of the comforter. She climbed on after, claiming the left side of my mattress, my side of the bed. "I think I should ruin all her clothes as a favor," Margaret continued. "She'd love to be obligated to buy a new wardrobe."

I scooted onto the right side of the bed, the side tucked into the room's corner, where Margaret always slept when she slept over. From there, I could see us both reflected in the mirror on the opposite wall, so I shook out my hair and arranged my limbs a little more artfully. Margaret, whose eyes sought out reflective surfaces at least as often as mine, looked over her shoulder into the mirror, caught what I was doing, and began to do the same.

She extended her neck and bent up her right leg, which lay on top of her left, to raise her hip, so her waist became a curved shape. We moved in silence, making these minor adjustments, until the picture of ourselves we saw in the mirror appeared desirable, composed—establishing whatever we said next as a conversation had by attractive people sitting attractively.

"We have a topic," I said, a little salaciously. Salaciousness felt like the only tone I knew how to take.

"We have a real topic!" Margaret echoed, with a coy little move of the chin. She seemed unusually alert, like she wanted her wits about her. For once, I'd done something Margaret hadn't already done herself. I'd hooked up with a girl, with Eleanor, a person we'd both seen naked and whose mother we knew, Eleanor, who had been but was no longer equally our other best friend. Now Eleanor was my girlfriend. Now both of Margaret's best friends were dating each other.

"So how was it?" she asked.

I realized I couldn't continue in the mode I'd begun—I couldn't *gossip* about hooking up with Eleanor—but I didn't know how to reply otherwise.

"Good," I said, and I could tell Margaret thought this was for dramatic effect, misreading me.

She rolled her eyes. "I'm so glad," she said, meaning *Say the rest already.*

But I didn't know how. If I were Margaret, or rather if Eleanor had been some boy, I would have gotten us both on the floor. I'd have sat us on our knees to show Margaret how my right knee slowly moved between Eleanor's legs as we kissed and touched each other, so that eventually she'd sat on my thigh and began to grind herself against me. But this information was private, I felt sure—the way Eleanor had stopped, embarrassed, because rubbing yourself on someone's thigh wasn't the kind of sexual experience any of us anticipated having or heard about as an achievement. I couldn't tell Margaret about either Eleanor's pleasure or her embarrassment.

"Well, what's a pussy like?" Margaret tried.

Though I appreciated the way she framed the question, I couldn't speak in general without speaking about Eleanor. I had a sample size of one.

"Really soft," I said.

I felt a rising tide of anxiety, perhaps the same fear that had stopped me from talking to Margaret in the first place. How would our friendship be, from now on, if I couldn't reveal every inch of my life to her, without consideration for other people, the way we always had? Could I keep telling her how hot she was every time she tried on a new outfit? Could I keep letting her borrow all my clothes, or would it upset Eleanor to see Margaret braless in my sweaters? Could we keep showering together? Could we keep loving each other in all the ways we always had?

"Did you like, make her come?" Margaret asked, still seeking a point of entry for this conversation. She'd begun to seem nervous. She checked the lock screen of her phone and then put it to sleep again. I didn't want to make her nervous. Having surpassed or at least exited the realm of her experience made me feel like I was living my own life, but it also made me feel lonely. I wondered if Margaret would ever hook up with a girl. I wondered if Margaret had kissed Eleanor even a little bit for the sake of catching up with me.

"I don't think so," I replied.

"Oh."

"I mean, I didn't either," I said with some trepidation. A thin wind blew through the room, air cool and light like I hadn't felt since the start of the season.

"Right."

"I think either of us coming would have been hard, though, on our first try." This seemed like a kind of truth I could convey, something I could tell Margaret that was real but didn't seem to compromise Eleanor.

"Oh, yeah, totally, of course," she reassured me. "It's not like a boy has ever made me come."

Which wasn't something Margaret had ever acknowledged to me before. Her stories typically conveyed a certain smugness about how she'd made the other person feel, how she'd done such a great job getting them to ejaculate as planned, but she skipped over saying much about her own pleasure. She told me if she liked it or not, but she didn't treat her physical experience as the point. When she confessed this to me, I heard in her voice such an evident desire to rescue me from even the potential of my own doubt about my sexual performance that at last I identified a place I could begin.

"Do you want me to tell you something?"

"Yes," she said, at full attention. "Tell me."

"Before I went over, like when I knew I was going over to her house in an hour, I looked up clitorises. Like, I looked up *what is a clitoris* to be sure. And did you know, it's actually not only the little flesh at the top? That's just the most obvious part. It's also underneath your skin along the sides. It's like a wishbone shape around like the opening."

Margaret looked stricken. "Wait," she said. "What do you mean the flesh and what do you mean the sides?"

"Like the nub, the thing at the top."

Margaret sat up. "I don't know if I have that."

"You definitely have it. You'd know by now if you didn't have it."

She ran a hand through her hair. "I don't think I do."

"Okay, well, you've like had an orgasm," I said in a conciliatory, stating-the-facts tone of voice, because Margaret had previously led me to believe she knew how to make herself come, even if no one else did.

She demurred. "The thing is, I'm not sure if I have or not."

"Okay, but you told me about the faucet and the bathtub. You started when you were seven. I remember."

"Yeah, I know, but just because I touch myself doesn't mean that like anything especially happens. It just feels good and then eventually I stop."

This meant hooking up with Eleanor hadn't been the first thing I'd done before Margaret, only the first I knew about. She looked upset to have admitted this. She didn't want it to be true. She told me now because she needed me to have all the evidence, so I could assist her in sorting through it. Disclosure from Margaret made me feel vital, important.

"Yeah, totally, I know what you mean," I said, to comfort her. I showed her the diagram I'd found on an online encyclopedia. I'd saved a screenshot to my camera roll for future reference. The clitoris was an upside-down pink Y, the stem of the letter folded over at the top.

"What if I don't have that, Mina—and I can't?"

"Can't what?"

"Ever come."

"You have it."

"I don't think I do." Real fear cracked in her voice. I wanted to reassure Margaret, but for a moment, the urgency and sincerity of her worry broke through my confidence. I didn't know whether or not her anatomy was like mine. Then, determined, I bricked up this uncertainty, the way Margaret always did for me, when I needed her composure. It was my turn to be steadfast.

"I'm going to search if you can be born without a clitoris," she said rashly.

"No. Don't do that," I said with authority, my hand cutting her off. "Definitely, we're not doing that as a first step. That's a trap."

"Well, I need to know like right now."

I understood. "Do you want me to look?"

"Yes," she said. "Will you?"

I left to fetch a cotton swab. Margaret took off her pants and underwear and lay down on my bed, on top of the covers. This wasn't the first time I'd seen her vagina, though never from this angle and never so on purpose, with her legs half open, the overhead light on, my bedside table cloud lamp lit up, and the flashlight on Margaret's phone active and in her hand in case I needed additional light. We were apparently concerned I could be led astray by insufficient illumination, as though this were a mining expedition.

I was a little, though not painfully, embarrassed. I was pleased to be needed on a mission that could be entrusted to no one else. I was curious to know what she looked like. I felt no need to touch her, however. She was an attractive person, and I saw and loved her attractiveness, but her beauty had nothing to do with me, not in the way that Eleanor's did. Margaret naked was Margaret naked. We'd been naked together routinely for most of our lives. All that had changed was the understanding that I could have felt differently. Her clitoris was there, though its apex looked more like two soft sheets crossing over each other than the dense doubled-over rose I knew from my own.

"Are you sure?" she asked.

I pressed on the top with the cotton swab.

"Oh," she said, surprised.

Then I faintly traced down the sides, to explain the wishbone. She made a little shiver. This was the only thing I feared I shouldn't have seen. My heart sped for a second. Quickly, I withdrew my hand. "It's under there."

"That's crazy," she said, with a laugh, still holding on to her knees, unembarrassed to be naked or by her own reaction. "That's crazy!"

"I know," I agreed. "Like who was going to tell us that and when?" Relief at Margaret's relaxed response thumped through me. It felt right. This was our friendship, the ability to bare ourselves to each other.

She put her pants back on, and while she was getting dressed, she said, "I realize that might have been weird for you. Was that something we shouldn't have done—because of El, I mean?"

Margaret asked me this question over her shoulder and only after we'd already finished. I wondered when it had occurred to her. I wondered if she'd wanted, on some level, to gauge my reaction, to figure out if I wanted anything from her other than what I'd always wanted, now that I'd made it clear what I wanted from Eleanor.

"No," I said. "I mean I guess it was a little weird, but only in the way that I noticed that, like, this is something that could be weird but actually isn't."

Margaret nodded. A different imbalance was on my mind, however, something else I thought had to be addressed for Margaret and Eleanor and me to knit ourselves together again.

"I think you should apologize to Eleanor," I said. "Like I think you should say I'm sorry out loud." The two of them wouldn't get there on their own. Eleanor wouldn't ask for an apology, and Margaret wouldn't acknowledge a wrong unless someone made her. "She kissed you in front of other people. She did you a favor that was counter to her personality."

Margaret disagreed. Reclothed, she hopped back on my bed. "Kissing people you wouldn't kiss otherwise is literally the premise of Truth or Dare."

"Yes, but you took her participation for granted," I said. "It's Eleanor. She could have declined or left. She chose not to leave you hanging."

What I didn't say was that Eleanor kissing Margaret had been a betrayal of Eleanor's feelings for me, for Margaret's benefit. Did Margaret know that? We looked at each other. Margaret's eyes were brown, like mine, though lighter.

"Okay," she said, in the way that meant, *I'll do this because you're telling me to.*

"Okay," I said, in the way that meant, *Thank you for letting me determine what's necessary under our present circumstances.*

ALL SUMMER I'D REFUSED TO PULL UP WEEDS, AND ALL SUMMER my mom had let me refuse because she didn't want to pull them up either.

As a child, I'd found the task of weeding to be a source of deep confusion. About every plant, I'd ask my mother, "What about this one? Is this a weed?"

Years into my assisting her in the garden, she identified my misunderstanding. "A weed isn't a specific plant or group of plants. A weed is whatever you didn't plant in the garden on purpose."

I pointed to a tiny purple flower growing between two bricks in the pathway.

"It's not a weed if you don't want to remove it," she said.

The dense border of nodding thistle that always showed up along the edge of our backyard required no clarification, however. The plants were between four and five feet tall. Their roots extended an arm's length into the earth, and their pink heads drooped with the weight of several thousand seeds. They had to be yanked up annually lest they overtake the yard.

"I wouldn't mind," I said.

"You'd mind," my mom said.

On one of the last days of summer, we went out there with shovels, clippers, leather-palmed gloves, and protective shirts that made us sweat. For each plant, I first cut off its flowering head. The head had to be immediately dropped into an orange plastic bucket, not laid on the grass to scatter its seeds.

My phone vibrated in my pocket, and I removed one glove to check it. In our private thread, Eleanor had texted me a picture of her and Margaret sitting side by side next to her pool.

hurry up & cum over, she said. *we're having fun without u.*

be patient, I texted back.

Margaret had apologized to Eleanor several days prior. Eleanor accepted and acted like the apology wasn't necessary. From this, Margaret understood that it was. Then Eleanor gave Margaret her own account of what had happened between us on her bedroom floor.

"Unfortunately, I didn't transcribe her customer testimonial," Margaret said, having called me on her walk home from Eleanor's house. "But I can report that you received a favorable review."

The idea of the two of them having this conversation did inflame my brain. I knew if I asked Margaret for further details, she'd give them to me, so I couldn't ask. Eleanor had to be able to tell Margaret about hooking up with me without worrying Margaret would immediately go tell me what she said, and I had to be able to talk to Margaret about hooking up with Eleanor without worrying she would immediately go tell Eleanor what I said. We needed new rules to protect us from ourselves. I heard Margaret pause for questions, and I imagined her disappointment when they didn't come.

"You'll have to keep both our secrets," I told her instead, with a sly lift in my voice. An honored role, I implied. The keeper of the keys. "You'll have to decide what you can tell me."

I knew I had her there. Margaret loved doling out the truth on her schedule and according to her judgment.

"If I must," she said, titillated.

Next I had to tell Eleanor the service I'd performed for Margaret. I explained in person, so I wouldn't be tortured by the length of time between her text messages.

"She wanted me to look at her—" I gestured. "I'm telling you because I want you to know that it had nothing to do with the way we are together."

El considered what I'd said. "Alright." She nodded, took a breath. "You don't have to like report to me about Margaret. I know that's how you guys are."

I held her hand. "Do you think we can have the same best friend?"

"She was always your best friend first."

"But she's yours too."

"Then yes," Eleanor said.

The August sun beamed down on my face in the backyard. I'd crossed over from uncomfortably hot into a clarifying sweat. Liquid dripped down my neck and chest, soaked my bra, tried to stick my protective shirt to my skin. I put the tip of my shovel into the dirt and stomped on its rim, driving the spade down into the earth. I repeated the process until a circle of indentation formed around the thistle. Then I got down on my knees, wrapped my arms around the base of the bristling plant, and yanked it from the ground in a painful embrace. The mass of spindly roots always resisted removal, clinging to the earth like a head of white hair. I had to sever the roots with clippers, careful to cut the central thread two inches below the crown, before tossing the body of the plant onto the lawn for later retrieval.

I removed one thistle and then another. The weeds tussled against my neck and shoulders, biting my exposed skin. I looked over at my mother, standing in a ring of cleared plants. She'd slowed down her pace. She had to stop after every thistle, put her hands on her hips, breathe deeply, and then start again. I saw her gathering up her will for the next weed.

"Go inside and sit," I said. She looked at the remaining weeds and considered whether or not she was willing to give up on them. "No," I said. "I mean—you rest, I'll finish." And when I did, I went inside and told her I had a girlfriend.

WE COMMEMORATED THE END OF SUMMER AT ELEANOR'S HOUSE, all of us actually in the pool instead of merely gathered around it. Margaret tied her hair on top of her head, so it wouldn't get wet. Eleanor wore a pair of goggles and her Alone Time necklace around her neck. I floated on a noodle.

"I walked in on my parents having sex," Margaret announced.

"What!" I exclaimed at the same time as Eleanor demanded, "When?" and made a splash.

Margaret glamorously raised a hand to shield her face. "Yesterday." She deposited the word. "No plan to get back together. They signed their divorce papers and were feeling nostalgic."

"These people!" I said in my own removed tone of displeasure, because that was what Margaret's delivery seemed to call for.

"They could have at least absconded to a hotel for their wrongdoing," Eleanor agreed, sensing the same.

"Well, they locked the door to my mom's office. I literally got out the key and unlocked it."

"You did?" I asked, a little shocked, even for Margaret.

"They didn't deserve to pretend they were getting away with it." A momentary silence followed this statement, which Margaret cut through by dunking herself underwater. She came back up in a rush, dark hair plastered to her cheeks and neck. "What if you guys break up?" she asked, looking at neither of us. Eleanor's and my eyes met in alarm. My heart began to percuss. Then Margaret threw her head back into the pool, hair underwater, face a flat oval up to the sky, and groan-shouted in the silliest, almost operatic voice, "What if *all* my parents get divorced?"

This idea of Margaret being our baby made us start laughing and laughing, a little hysterically, because once we stopped, we'd have to answer her or stand there in silence. Eleanor bounced up and down off the bottom of the pool.

"I don't know!" she said.

I didn't know either. I'd hardly even asked myself the question. I felt attacked by Margaret suddenly shouting my inner fears into the ether while I bobbed nearby on a pool noodle. But she'd yelled them at the three of us, all together, and the alchemy of our friendship stirred in response.

"We'll fight over you," I said, a rush of adrenaline slinging through me, prickling in my armpits. "But we won't make you testify."

Eleanor nodded in her goggles. "We'll buy you so many presents, but we won't make you say mean things about us to each other."

"You promise?" Margaret asked.

ON THE LAST NIGHT BEFORE school, Eleanor posted a picture of the three of us—me in the middle, Margaret with her arm around my waist, and Eleanor on my other side, licking my cheek. I cradled my phone in my hand, my face on my pillow. I thought of all the photos the three of us had ever taken, ever made visible on the internet. I wondered if anyone would be able to tell what the picture meant about who we were to each other by looking at it. At least by then we knew.

THESE LINES ARE DRAWN AND REDRAWN—WHO IS WHAT AND TO whom. I loved Eleanor, and I loved Margaret. I love them still. We live in different cities now, visit for birthdays, talk on the phone. Margaret calls me almost daily, at whatever hour she tires of the mundane.

"Why am I not famous?" she sometimes says, as soon as I pick up the phone. "Where is my world renown?"

Eleanor calls less often and in the middle of the night.

"Remember when I used to take your underwear," she'll say. "From your dresser, and wear them to school?" She doesn't have any roommates, because her parents pay her rent. Sometimes she spends too many days in a row alone in her apartment. Then she wants to talk for hours, reminisce.

Now we know about missing each other, having friends who haven't met our mothers. Now a week apart or a month isn't very long at all. In each other's absence, we feel an absence of ourselves as well. I want to be the Mina I am for Margaret, for Eleanor, the self I occupy uniquely in their presence. I know they want the same when they call me—to remember who they are through how I see them. I can do that, I say, as I offer their shimmering reflection. I can be a mirror who loves you.

Acknowledgments

This book exists thanks to a network of support. Thank you, Alexa Stark, for your excellent judgment and vision. Thank you, Katy Nishimoto, for showing me how to close the gap between what *Girl's Girl* was and what it could become. Thank you, JP Woodham. Thank you, Cassie Vu, Debbie Aroff, Donna Cheng, Georgia Brainard, Leah Sims, Luke Epplin, Lynn Wu, Michelle Jasmine, Susan Turner, Corina Diez, Will Lyman, Talia Cieslinski, Whitney Frick, and the entire team at The Dial Press for bringing *Girl's Girl* to readers.

Thank you, Lynn Steger Strong. In your class, my book became a book. Thank you to my classmates: Ben Constantino, Ben Izzo, Deena Drewis, Jean Kawahara, Kristin Koval, Peter Mayshle, Sarah Kasbeer, Shari MacDonald Strong, and especially Lacey Dunham, Nicole VanderLinden, and Xian Chiang-Waren for the many extracurricular calls that helped me hold this whole book in my head.

Thank you, Literary Cleveland, for supporting *Girl's Girl* and the writers in our city. Thank you, Matt Weinkam and Michelle Smith. Thank you, Laura Maylene Walter and Andrea Imdacha, for our community of three.

Thank you to my professors at Washington University in St.

Louis and the University of Chicago who drew out my enthusiasm with their own, especially David Lawton for his time and mentorship. Thank you, Anna, for letting me read the whole book to you out loud. Thank you to the Bread Loaf, Sewanee, and Disquiet literary conferences for supporting my development as a writer. Thank you to VCCA for time and space.

Thank you to all my girl loves. You made me and this book real. Thank you, Lindsay, for living through the impossible era of fifteen with me and every impossible era since. Thank you, Madeleine, for our lifetime of perfect conversations. You both taught me how to write *Girl's Girl*.

Thank you to my family, Feldman and Myers. Thank you, Gloria, Micaela, and Michael. Thank you, Carolyn. Thank you, Lizzy. Thank you, Lois. Thank you, Will and Ani. Thank you, Rob. I love you, and the rest is private. Thank you to my mom and dad, Catherine and Edward. I owe you who I am.

About the Author

Sonia Feldman lives in Cleveland, Ohio. She won the PEN/Robert J. Dau Short Story Prize for Emerging Writers, and her poetry and fiction have appeared in *The Missouri Review, The Southern Review,* and *Waxwing*. She also runs Sonia's Poem of the Week, a popular email newsletter. *Girl's Girl* is her first novel.

soniacfeldman.com
Instagram: @writsonia

About the Type

This book was set in Fairfield, the first typeface from the hand of the distinguished American artist and engraver Rudolph Ruzicka (1883–1978). Ruzicka was born in Bohemia (in the present-day Czech Republic) and came to America in 1894. He set up his own shop, devoted to wood engraving and printing, in New York in 1913 after a varied career working as a wood engraver, in photoengraving and banknote printing plants, and as an art director and freelance artist. He designed and illustrated many books, and was the creator of a considerable list of individual prints—wood engravings, line engravings on copper, and aquatints.